Only for the Season

D.E. Haggerty

Also by D.E. Haggerty

Chapter 1

Jeremy – a billionaire who's beginning to regret his decision to visit Smuggler's Hideaway for the holidays

JEREMY

"Turn left in fifty feet on Treasure Trap Trail."

"Left? Where? Treasure Trap Trail?" I search the area, but there's no road to the left. There's only a dirt trail. Am I supposed to drive on it?

"Turn left here."

"I'm turning already."

I'm also talking to my GPS as if it's human. I blame my isolation for the past weeks, trying to get this new app developed for my company, *Apparoo.* It's been tough not having anyone to talk to. But I also haven't vented my frustration on anyone, so HR should be happy with me.

My rental car bumps down the dirt road. Why in the world does Eli live on a dirt road? As the co-founder of *Apparoo,* he has enough money to pave all the roads on this island.

Why the hell does he want to live on Smuggler's Hideaway anyway? An island is nice for a vacation. Not as somewhere to live.

Baa!

"Shit!" I yell and slam on the brakes before I hit the sheep in the middle of the road. Where the hell did it come from?

My heart batters in my chest as the car screeches to a halt inches from the animal. I'm not an animal lover, but I don't want to kill some innocent beast.

I wait, but it doesn't move. I honk my horn. The sheep still doesn't move.

Great. Just what I need.

I roll down my window and shout at it. "Move on. Get out of here."

Awesome. Now I'm shouting at some random sheep on a dirt road in the middle of nowhere. Can this day get any worse?

The sheep starts to move. Good. I can get out of here. But instead of wandering away, it turns around to fully face me. *Baa!*

Damnit. I fold out of the car.

"Go! Move!"

Baa!

"Don't you baa me. This is a road for cars. Not a road for animals."

Baa!

Screw this. I'm not getting into a fight with a sheep. I climb back in the car. There's no way Eli lives on this road. I'll turn around and drive back into town to get directions.

I turn the steering wheel fully to the left to drive across the road. I barely make it a foot before I reach the edge. Shit. Turning around on this narrow road is going to be impossible. I'll have to reverse the entire way.

Stupid sheep. Stupid island. Stupid app I can't figure out how to program.

I slowly reverse down the road. The sheep continues to bleat as I drive.

"I'm going already!" I shout at it.

I'm almost at the main road when I notice a man walking through the field. Is he the sheep herder? Do sheep herders still exist? Whatever.

"Hey!" I shout to get the man's attention.

He waves and continues on his way.

"Hey!" I shout again. "Can you help me?"

He switches direction and makes his way toward me. "Your fancy car break down?" He lifts his ball cap to scratch his forehead. "I'm not any good with cars but my brother is. Do you want me to call him?"

"The car is fine, but I'm lost."

He smirks. "I kind of figured as much when I saw you driving down the animal trail."

"Animal trail?"

His nose wrinkles as he stares down at me. "A trail for animals."

I growl. "I know what an animal trail is."

"You seemed confused."

"Because my GPS sent me down this road."

"GPS doesn't work on Smuggler's Hideaway."

I frown. "GPS works everywhere unless the signal is obstructed or weakened. This includes indoors due to thick walls or metal roofs, underwater, underground, or in areas with dense tree coverage."

He lifts his hands in the air. "Okay, Mr. GPS Expert. You believe what you want to, but I'm telling you, GPS doesn't work on Smuggler's Hideaway."

This is ridiculous. There aren't GPS black holes. It's a—

What am I doing? Arguing with a sheep herder about how GPS works is not going to help me find Eli's house.

"Do you know Eli Raider?"

"Maybe."

"I'm trying to find his house."

His eyes narrow. "You're not a reporter, are you?"

"I am not a reporter."

He studies me for a moment before nodding. "Okay. You take a left here. Drive about half a mile. Turn right at the mermaid monument. His house is at the end of the street. You can't miss it."

"Thank you."

"Welcome to Smuggler's Hideaway," he replies before ambling away.

I finish reversing down the animal trail – I should have known something was up when the GPS called the road the Treasure Trap Trail – and take a left. I drive half a mile, and sure enough, there's a mermaid monument.

I turn right. I frown when I notice the sign for *Mermaid Mystical Gardens*. I don't know what mystical gardens are, but it appears I'm going to find out anyway. Less than a minute later, the road opens onto a parking lot. Not a small parking lot for Eli's house. A huge parking lot filled to the brim.

I pull to the side. Crowds are making their way to the entrance of what appears to be an amusement park.

What the hell? Did the sheep herder send me on a wild goose chase?

Enough of this. I was trying to surprise Eli with my visit. He invited me to celebrate Thanksgiving with his family. I initially told him no, but then I got stuck on the coding of the new app and needed a break.

I thought a trip to Smuggler's Hideaway would get the creative juices flowing again. Not thus far.

I dial Eli's number and listen to the phone ring over the speakers. And ring. And ring.

"You've reached Eli Raider."

I hit disconnect. His voicemail won't give me directions to his house.

I whirl the car around and drive toward Smuggler's Rest – the town I drove through when I first arrived on the island. Someone there must know Eli and where he lives. The place isn't very big after all. And Eli is a billionaire.

When I arrive at the main shopping street, I notice most of the stores are already closed. I search for any business with its lights on. Aha! There.

I park in front of the building. *Pirate's Pastries.* Is everything on this island pirate or mermaid themed?

I frown when I reach the door. The lights are on, but the sign says 'closed'.

I knock on the door. I wait but when no one answers, I knock again and shout, "Hello! Is anyone in there?"

The door behind the counter swings open, and a woman hurries out. Her cheeks are flushed, flour dusts her hair like a scattering of snow, and the messy pile of hair on top of her head shows off the graceful line of her neck and the sharp cut of her cheekbones. As she comes closer, I notice the clear, bright blue of her eyes and the playful tilt of her nose.

My gaze drops to her body. She has curves for days. Another man might think she's chubby, but I think she's perfect. Things are looking up.

She points to the sign. "We're closed."

"I just have a question."

"If it's about your order, it'll be ready on time."

"It's not about an order."

She plants her hands on her hips. "What's it about?"

I point to the door. "Can you open this up?"

She frowns. "Do I look like an idiot to you?"

"No."

"Then, you should understand why I'm not opening up the door to a strange man I've never met before."

"I'm not here to hurt you."

"Said by every man in the world seconds before he decides to hurt someone. Usually a woman."

"Fine," I grumble. "Can you give me directions to Eli Raider's house?"

Her eyes narrow. "Do you know Eli?"

"He's my friend." I'm not telling her my name. I don't need another woman to fall all over me because of my money. Been there. Done that. Have the t-shirt to prove it.

"Sorry, friend, I can't give you directions."

"You don't know where he lives?"

"Not what I said."

"I have his address. I just need directions because apparently, GPS doesn't work on this Podunk island."

"If we're such a Podunk island, you'll be able to find his house on your own."

"I tried. A sheep tried to kill me and then some sheep herder sent me to an amusement park."

She giggles, and despite how annoyed I am, I can't help but think the sound is lovely. "Call Eli. If you're such good friends, he'll give you directions."

"I tried. He's not answering his phone."

She digs into the pocket of her apron. She pulls a measuring spoon, pastry brush, and sifter out before shouting, "Aha!" and flourishing her phone. She puts the phone on speaker before dialing.

"Hey, Parker. What's up?" Eli answers.

"Your so-called friend is here and he can't find your house."

He groans. "You know what to do."

"Gotcha." She hangs up.

I smile at her. "Directions, please."

She smirks. "Sure. You drive out of town for about a mile and turn right at the mermaid statue."

I groan. She's sending me on a wild goose chase. The same way the sheep herder did.

"What is wrong with the people on this island?"

"Maybe you should leave the island and then you won't have to deal with us." With those words, she pivots on her heel and marches away.

I bury my face in my hands. Why did I think visiting Eli would help me get over my coder's block? Things aren't looking up after all.

Chapter 2

Parker – a baker who is beginning to hate the smell of pumpkin pie

PARKER

A knock on the back door of the bakery startles me awake.

"Go away," I shout. "I'm not giving you directions."

I lay my head back on the table. I just need a few more minutes of sleep and then I'll get back to baking. I promise.

"Parker. It's me. Holly."

I groan. So much for getting a few more minutes of sleep. Holly works the counter in the bakery. If she's here, it's time to open up.

My back and knees crack as I stand and make my way to the door. I open it and usher Holly inside before locking it again.

I usually keep the door open during the day, but with some weirdo wandering around town trying to find Eli, I don't dare. It's not the first time a reporter has come to Smuggler's Hideaway to find Eli. Eli's a billionaire who co-founded *Apparoo* – a tech company – and owns *Buccaneer's Whiskey & Distillery.*

The media is fascinated by him. His fiancée, Paisley, just had a baby and the gossip magazines are willing to pay big bucks for a picture of baby Stephanie. Not on my watch.

"Geez, boss lady, did you fall asleep while baking again?" Holly brushes flour off my face while giggling.

"Today is Thanksgiving. Everyone and their uncle ordered some kind of pie for their holiday dinner."

Thank the mermaids. Business hasn't been great since a chain coffee shop opened up on the boardwalk two years ago. I could use some extra income to get me through the winter months when the tourism on the island slows to a crawl.

"My parents are pissed at me for working today."

I frown. Shit. I didn't think about Holly missing Thanksgiving with her family to work today. I avoid my family as much as possible. There won't be a Shaw family Thanksgiving to attend.

At least I don't live at home with them anymore. Talk about uncomfortable. I used to live in the loft above the bakery, but then I had it renovated to rent out to tourists. I can't afford to miss the income from the rent, so I moved back home for a while.

Now I have my own place. Well, not exactly my own since I have a roommate. And it's not what anyone would call a 'nice' place, but it's free of my parents and their judginess.

"Go on home," I tell Holly. "I'll handle the front."

She lifts her eyebrows. "While you bake?"

"Sure."

"Do you not remember what happened the last time you tried to handle the front while baking?"

"Maybe I wanted the fire department to come." I wiggle my eyebrows. "The new recruit is pretty cute."

She rolls her eyes. "Oh, please. You complained non-stop about how they overreacted."

"They totally did."

"The smoke alarms went off."

"Fire does not always follow smoke."

"Your Blackbeard's revenge cookies were burnt to a crisp."

"But there was no fire."

"Whatever," she mumbles. "It's time to open."

She pushes through the door to the front, but I chase after her. "I'm serious, Holly. You should go home."

She motions toward the door where a line of customers has formed. "No way. You're too busy baking pies to handle customers today."

"I can do it."

"Don't you have to deliver all those pies before noon?"

Crap on a rusty smuggler's ship. I did promise to deliver all the pies this morning. What was I thinking? I wasn't thinking. I was envisioning dollar signs.

"I don't want you to miss Thanksgiving with your family."

"We don't eat until this afternoon." She grins. "Mom's just mad because I can't help in the kitchen this morning because I'm here."

"In other words, you should thank me."

She rolls her eyes as she hurries to the door to open the bakery. "Good morning. Who's ready for some pastries this morning?"

I leave her to it and return to the kitchen to finish the Thanksgiving pie orders.

"Parker!" Holly shouts sometime later.

I sigh. She usually only asks me to come to the front if someone's complaining. She doesn't handle criticism. But she doesn't mind soaking up all the comments about my baked goodies.

I force myself to smile before joining her. "How can I help?"

She motions to the customer at the front of the line. "Sloane wants to order a pie. For today."

"Sorry, Sloane. I stopped accepting Thanksgiving orders last week."

"But you don't understand."

I do understand. I've known Sloane since we were both kids running around the island getting into trouble for tormenting the tourists by giving them false directions and winding them up about 'mermaid' sightings.

Which is why I know she probably forgot all about the holiday until she woke up this morning and saw the Macy's Thanksgiving Day Parade on her television. Sloane doesn't understand the concept of keeping an agenda. Let alone, actually referring to it from time to time.

"Even if I wanted to help you out, I can't. I have dozens of pies I need to deliver before noon. I don't have time to bake you a pie."

She pouts. "But it's me."

"Buy some pumpkin pie cookies instead," the woman in line behind her says.

I wave to Jade. "Are you here to pick up your pecan pie?"

"And about five dozen cookies before Adrian eats me out of house and home. I love my son, but it's not fair how much he can eat. I so much as peek at a cookie and I gain five pounds."

"Tell me about it." My hips could have their own zip codes. "Let me grab your pie while Holly packs up your cookies."

"What about my pie?" Sloane hollers.

"It's waiting for you at the grocery store."

"Their pies don't taste orgasmic."

Holly giggles. I slam my hands over her ears. "You need to find a man or woman to satisfy your sexual needs because my pie won't be helping."

Holly slaps my hands away. "You're worse than my mom. I know what an orgasm is for mermaid's sake. I'm nineteen. I might have had one myself."

I groan. "Please don't tell your mom you're sexually active. She'll blame me."

I can't afford to lose Holly. She's a great worker. Always arrives on time. Willing to stay late when I need her to. Her friends occasionally show up and she gives them freebies until the display case is empty, but it's a small price to pay for a good worker.

I grab Jade's pie from the kitchen. It's all wrapped up and ready to go.

"Here you go," I hand her the pie while covertly scanning the bakery for signs of Sloane.

"She's gone," Jade says. "Holly read her the riot act for bothering you on a holiday after you've been baking all night and she slinked away with her tail between her legs."

"Okay."

She narrows her eyes on me. "You were already thinking about ways to bake her a pie, weren't you?"

I shrug. There's no sense denying it. I have a problem saying no to my friends. And an even bigger problem with my bank account.

"You should—" She's cut off when someone screams.

"I saw a rat!"

Jade mumbles goodbye before rushing out of the bakery, leaving me to deal with a hysterical customer.

"There isn't a rat," I tell the woman. I don't know her, so she must be a tourist. All the smugglers know there isn't a rat in my bakery. But there might be a furry animal.

She points to the corner. "I saw it with my very own eyes."

I sigh before marching to the display case and grabbing a few Selkie bites. They're mini cookies made of sea salt and dark chocolate chips. They're divine. My oversized behind is the proof.

"Viking," I holler. "I have your favorite."

He peeks out from behind a chair.

"Oh my word." The woman clutches her chest. "You have a pet rat."

"Viking is not a rat. He's an otter."

"Like an otter is so much better. I can't believe I came in here. I'll be going to the coffee shop on the boardwalk from now on." She whirls away and scurries out of the bakery.

I scan the line of waiting customers. All of them are locals and not bothered one bit by the appearance of Viking. Of course, they know the otter lives with me. He's the mascot for Smuggler's Rest – the largest town on the island of Smuggler's Hideaway.

The other two towns on the island – Pirate's Perch and Rogue's Landing – have live mascots as well. Plank, the foul-mouthed parrot, is the mascot for Pirate's Perch. And Rogue's Landing has Rogue, the naughty raccoon that's addicted to marshmallows.

Usually, the location of the mascots is kept secret since it's tradition for smugglers to try and steal the mascots in the summer. But no one is taking Viking from me. I love the furry guy and I'm not letting him go.

I kneel in front of Viking. "Here you go." I feed him a bit of the Selkie bite. "Did the mean tourist scare you?"

I understand. I nearly peed my pants when the reporter banged on my door last night. I won't be forgetting to switch off the lights in the bakery while I'm baking in the kitchen again.

Chapter 3

"Next time I need a break, I'm going to a spa. Alone."

JEREMY

"Good morning."

At Eli's greeting, I glance up from my computer. "Morning," I mumble.

He lifts up his coffee cup. "Need a refill?"

I slide my cup across the kitchen counter toward him in answer.

"Paisley is happy you decided to accept my invitation for Thanksgiving," he says as he prepares our coffee. "Although a little heads up would have been nice."

I shrug. "I was trying to surprise you."

He chuckles. "And ended up getting lost on Smuggler's Hideaway."

I grunt. "I didn't expect the locals to send me on a wild goose chase."

"They thought you were a reporter and were protecting me. No way was anyone – especially Parker – going to give you directions."

Parker. Despite how annoying she was – giving me wrong directions is not very neighborly – I can't get her beautiful face or smile out of my mind. And those curves? My fingers itch to touch them. My cock twitches. It wants in on the fun.

No one is having any fun, I remind my body. I'm here to finish coding the app. I'm not here to seduce a local.

Why can't we do both?

I ignore my cock. I've learned my lesson about listening to it. Nothing good comes from being led around by my dick.

Eli sets a coffee in front of me and sits on the stool next to mine. "So, what's up?"

I feign innocence. "What do you mean, what's up?"

He barks out a laugh. "I have five brothers who are all shit stirrers to their core, I know better than to buy your innocent look."

I try batting my lashes.

"You can't fool me. I've known you since the first day of freshman orientation when you arrived in our dorm room wearing a Darth Vader outfit."

"I was not wearing a Darth Vader outfit." It was a t-shirt of Darth Vader. Not the same thing.

He raises his eyebrow. "My brother has the same t-shirt."

I leap at the chance to change the subject. "How is Jaxon doing?"

He shakes a finger at me. "Nope. I'm not allowing you to avoid my questions."

"What questions?"

He scowls. "Jeremy, what are you doing on Smuggler's Hideaway?"

"I'm here to celebrate Thanksgiving with your family."

"One, you hate celebrating holidays with family. You prefer to pick up a supermodel and spend the weekend between the sheets. Two, you hate small towns. I believe you refer to them as 'Podunk'."

I can't contradict him since he's right. I do hate celebrating holidays with my family. I swallow the growl trying to emerge at the thought of my so-called family.

But I'm done with supermodels. They're clingy and only want one thing. My money. I want someone to want me for me. Not because of how many zeroes are in my bank account. But I've given up on that particular dream.

What about Parker? She didn't care about your money. She also doesn't know who I am. Everything changes once women know my name.

"Jeremy," Eli pushes.

I clear my throat and push all my thoughts away. "I needed a break from California."

His eyes narrow. "And why did you need a break?"

I shrug. "Just tired of all the California bullshit."

"You always were a crappy liar."

I glare at him. "I am not a crappy liar."

"You scratch your neck when you lie."

"I do not…" Damn. I am scratching my neck. I drop my hand. "Whatever."

"Tell me what's going on. Paisley says I'm a great listener."

"Paisley never said you were a great listener."

The door to the kitchen flies open and Paisley rushes in, cradling a baby. "I never said what?"

"You had to marry a woman with the hearing of a bat," I mutter.

"One, we're not married. And, two, bats cannot hear the best of all animals. The greater wax moth can. And, three, what were you discussing?"

Eli stands and takes the baby from Paisley. The love on his face has my stomach souring. I want a family. People who will love me for who I am. But experience has taught me the truth. People don't love you for who you are when you're a billionaire.

Eli found a unicorn in Paisley. The chances of me finding another unicorn are nearly non-existent.

"We were discussing work," Eli says to Paisley before kissing her forehead.

"Which is code for 'it's none of my business'. Fine, I'll drop it." Yep, Paisley is a unicorn. Any other woman would pry and pry.

Paisley digs around in the back of the refrigerator before pulling out a bottle. "You're feeding Stephanie this morning. I need to cook and get the house ready."

Eli scowls. "I told you to have the food catered."

Paisley's lips purse. "I am not having the food catered at the first Thanksgiving we host."

"It's too much for you."

Paisley slams the bottle on the counter before turning to Eli and spitting daggers out of her eyes at him. Uh oh. This is my cue to exit the kitchen.

I shut my computer and gather my things. But before I can pick everything up, Eli shoves the baby at me.

"Here. Take her."

I hold up my hands. "I don't know how to hold a baby."

"It's easy. Make sure her neck and head are cradled. Treat her like she's the most precious thing on earth."

Most precious thing on earth? This is not a responsibility I can handle.

"Nope. You can hold her and fight with your wife about what an idiot you are at the same time."

"Thank you, Jeremy." Paisley beams at me. "I knew there was a reason I liked you."

"Seriously?" Eli asks. "You're taking her side?"

"I'm not taking sides at all." I keep my hands in the air as I back away. I can rescue my computer later. It's not as if I was actually getting any coding done anyway. "But I know better than to tell a woman things are too much for her."

Eli growls. "It's my job to protect Paisley."

"Your job? I'm a job now?"

"Fine. My privilege. It's my privilege to protect Paisley. Happy now?" He waits for her to nod before continuing. "What kind of protector would I be if I allowed her to run herself ragged this soon after birth? We have fourteen guests coming. It's too much."

"Hold up. Fourteen guests?" I was expecting a small, intimate Thanksgiving. I have no desire to answer the numerous questions people always have about me once they realize who I am.

"My mom and step-dad. My brother Rhett with his fiancée and their two children. My brother Jaxon and his wife Blossom. My brother Kai and his girlfriend Harper, and her dad. My brother Zane and his baby, Adele. And Miles."

The tension in my chest loosens. It's Eli's family. They won't grill me with a thousand questions since they're used to having a billionaire around.

"I can cook for fourteen guests without a problem," Paisley declares.

Eli shoves baby Stephanie into my arms before stalking to Paisley.

My heart goes into overdrive while my chest tightens. I've never held a baby before. I don't want to drop her. If anything happens to Stephanie, Eli would kill me. Rightfully so.

"A little help here," I holler as the baby squirms in my arms.

Paisley frowns at Eli before making her way to me and retrieving the baby. "What are you thinking, Eli? He's obviously terrified of babies."

Eli shrugs. "He needs to get used to the idea."

"Get used to…" Paisley trails off to study me. "Is love in the air?"

I back away. "No. Love is not the air. Most definitely not."

"Why not?"

"You're a unicorn," I tell her. "There aren't any other women in the world who can see past the money to the man."

She fiddles with her glasses as she studies me. "Hmm…"

The scheming look in her eye is beginning to terrify me. "I need to…"

The doorbell rings. I smile. Perfect excuse.

"I'll get the door while the two of you discuss why Eli thinks you can't cook for fourteen people."

"I can cook for four thousand people if I want," Paisley says.

I chuckle as I make my way to the door. I open it and frown at the person waiting on the porch. "What are you doing here?"

Parker lifts the bag she's carrying. "Special Thanksgiving day delivery."

I nearly moan at the scent of pumpkin and cinnamon emitting from the bag. My stomach rumbles. I haven't eaten a homemade pumpkin pie in years. Mom stopped baking once she got her claws in my money.

"Are you going to stare at me all day, or are you going to take the pies?"

Chapter 4

"The only thing worse than a reporter? A billionaire."

PARKER

I hold my breath as I turn the corner in the van loaded with pies. When the turn is complete and none of the pies has flipped over or fallen to the floor, I blow out a breath.

Thank goodness. No disaster. And thank goodness I could borrow this van from the brewery. I don't think anyone expects Thanksgiving pies to be delivered in a *Five Fathoms Brewing* van, but this is Smuggler's Hideaway. Nothing is truly out of the ordinary here.

I slow to a stop in front of Jack and Lily Milton's house. I've known Jack and Lily since first grade. Their daughter, Sophia, was a year younger than me in school. We used to congregate in Lily's kitchen at the end of school. She made the best chocolate chip cookies. They were always hot out of the oven when we arrived.

I grab Lily's order – one Siren's Song Pumpkin Pie and one Blackbeard's Bourbon Chocolate Pie – before making my way to the front door.

"Lily! Jack!" I shout as I knock.

When no one answers the door, I check the time. I told them I'd arrive around eleven and it's five to the hour. They should be here.

I knock again. "Lily! Your pies are here!"

I'm contemplating leaving the pies on the porch when the door flies open.

"Hi, Parker." Lily's hair is a mess, and her blouse is buttoned wrong. Jack appears behind her. He's grinning. One guess what these two have been up to. I shouldn't be surprised. Lily and Jack never could keep their hands off each other.

My stomach sours. I want what they have. They met when Jack was working on the island and fell instantly in love – if the tales are to be believed.

But who wants a baker who has more curves than money and works more hours than there are in a day? No one, that's who.

I hand her the bag. "Here are your pies. Enjoy."

Lily's eyes light up. "We will. Your Blackbeard's Bourbon Chocolate Pie is downright sinful with its rich chocolate and whipped cream, and shaved dark chocolate topping."

I smile. I'm pretty proud of my pies. "Thank you."

I wave goodbye as I make my way back to the van to make my next delivery. I zigzag my way through Smuggler's Rest for the next hour. It's nearly noon when I realize I only have two deliveries to go – Eli and Mrs. Simpson.

I park in Mrs. Simpson's driveway and frown. The exterior needs a new coat of paint, but ever since Mr. Simpson died ten years ago, Mrs. Simpson hasn't been able to manage the work herself.

I carry Mrs. Simpson's pie to her front door. It opens before I reach it.

"Parker! How lovely to see you. Come in. Come in." She ushers me inside.

"I don't have much time. I have more pies to deliver," I tell her as I set the pie on her kitchen table, which is already set with plates and cups.

"Nonsense. You have time for a cup of coffee and a piece of pie."

This is the reason I saved her house for the second to last. She'd be the last, but Eli's house is out in the country.

"No coffee for me. I've had about ten cups already today."

"I'll put the kettle on for tea." She motions to the pie. "Go ahead and slice up two pieces."

I open the box and pick up the knife from the table. I take a moment to appreciate how pretty this Pearl Diver Pie is before I cut into it. It's vanilla bean cream pie with a white chocolate seashell on top and edible glitter pearls.

"Oh my, Parker. You've outdone yourself this time." She pats my hand. "Smuggler's Hideaway is lucky some fancy bakery in New York City didn't snap you up."

I could take or leave New York City. But, Paris, on the other hand? I've always dreamed of working there. And I nearly managed to. Unfortunately, nearly doesn't mean anything.

I slice two pieces and place them on plates while Mrs. Simpson prepares the tea.

"Sit. Sit." She indicates the chair and I settle in. There's no sense trying to rush her. She doesn't get much company and looks forward to Thanksgiving and my visit all year long. What kind of person would I be if I didn't stay a while?

"Tell me everything happening on Smuggler's Rest. And don't forget to tell me all about your young man."

"I don't have a man," I begin.

We chat for twenty minutes before I decide I need to go.

"It was lovely to see you, Mrs. Simpson. I'm off to deliver the last of my pies now."

"And then you can enjoy your Thanksgiving celebration as well."

I don't bother to tell her I won't be enjoying a celebration. Unless you consider sleeping after being awake for nearly two days a celebration. I guess it kind of is.

I blare music in the van as I drive toward Eli's. I will not fall asleep. I will not crash this van I do not own and dig myself deeper into debt.

I keep my eye out for Sammy the seal as I drive, but he's probably hiding somewhere warm since the weather has gotten colder. Not cold. It's never truly cold on Smuggler's Hideaway. Except for last year when we had the surprise snowstorm.

I shiver. I love snow, but I hope we don't have a surprise snowstorm this year. I can't afford for the electricity to go out and ruin all of my ingredients again.

I arrive at Eli's house – more mansion than house, really. This delivery bag is heavy since his fiancée, Paisley, ordered six pies.

I carefully make my way to their porch and knock on the door. It opens moments later, but it's not Eli or Paisley standing in the doorway. It's the man who stopped by the bakery looking for directions to this very house last night.

"What are you doing here?"

I was wondering the same about him, but instead of asking, I lift the bag of pies. "Special Thanksgiving day delivery."

His stomach growls, loud enough to make me smirk. My pies have a way of humbling even the most arrogant of men. Unfortunately, this particular rude one is also – now that I can see him clearly in the daylight – ridiculously attractive.

His dirty blond hair is an artful mess, the kind that makes my fingers twitch with the urge to touch it. His eyes – light brown and sharply focused – hold an intensity that hits me low in the belly. I wonder what they look like when he's lost in something... or someone.

He's all sharp lines and masculine angles: high cheekbones, a square jaw, and a chin marked with just the faintest dimple. Like the universe added a single flaw for balance. Except it doesn't work. The dimple only makes him more devastating.

Something stirs in my stomach – not hunger, not exactly. Butterflies, maybe. Or warning bells. Probably both. I remind myself he's a reporter. Trouble. Off-limits. No matter how good he looks.

"Are you going to stare at me all day, or are you going to take the pies?"

"What are you doing here?" he asks instead. "I thought you didn't know where Eli lived."

"I never said I didn't know where he lived."

"You gave me directions to *Mermaid Mystical Gardens.*"

I giggle. "Gets them every time."

Paisley rushes out of the kitchen. "Oh, good. You're here."

I lift the bag with pies again. This delivery is starting to feel like an upper-body workout. I am not kidding about how heavy these pies are.

"At your service. Holiday bliss in a bag."

She moans. "They smell delicious. Do you mind setting them out on the side table in the dining room?"

"Of course not." Good thing this is my last delivery.

I ignore the reporter and make my way to the dining room. Unfortunately, he doesn't ignore me. He follows me instead.

I set the bag on the table and lift out the first pie. I remove it from the box before setting it on the table.

"It's beautiful. What flavor is it?"

I don't hesitate to answer. Maybe he'll include *Pirate's Pastries* in his article about Eli. "It's Seafoam Meringue. A sea salt-caramel base with a torched blue-tinted meringue swirl."

"It looks like ocean waves."

I smirk. "And tastes like heaven."

He peeks into the bag. "What other pies do you have?"

"I didn't realize reporters were pie addicts."

He rears back. "Reporters? I'm not a reporter."

I snort. "Dude, you're literally in Eli's house to write a story about him. Of course, you're a reporter."

He sputters, but Eli strolls into the room before he can answer. "Hey, Parker."

"Is this baby Stephanie?" I squeal. "Can I hold her? Please."

The doorbell rings and he chuckles before handing the baby to me. "I'll be right back."

"Take your time," I mutter as I run a finger down Stephanie's nose. "Aren't you adorable? You're going to break all the smugglers' hearts when you get older."

The reporter snorts. "Typical woman. Give her a baby and she loses her mind."

"I hope you're a better reporter than you are human being."

"I'm not a reporter."

I roll my eyes. "Not with those observation skills you aren't."

His brow wrinkles. "Observation skills?"

"You said I'm losing my mind over a baby. Yes, baby Stephanie is adorable. But she's not the reason I'm happy. I'm happy because Eli and Paisley finally got over their decade-long feud and found their way to love. I'm happy Paisley finally has a family who deserves her."

Paisley rushes into the room. "Thank goodness. I thought I lost you." She steals Stephanie and rushes away but pauses before she exits. Her gaze bounces back and forth between me and the reporter.

"Have you two met before?"

"Yep. We met last night when he knocked on the bakery's door and asked for directions."

"Which you didn't give him."

"I know better than to give a reporter directions to your house."

She smirks. "Jeremy isn't a reporter. He's the co-founder of *Apparoo*."

"*Apparoo?*" As in the multi-billion-dollar tech empire? And he's the co-founder? Those butterflies in my stomach fall to their death. Billionaire is worse than reporter. Way worse.

Jeremy smirks as he extends his hand. "Told you I wasn't a reporter."

"You didn't tell me your name either."

I cross my arms over my chest and he drops his hand.

"I don't tell people my name."

I roll my eyes so hard I nearly fall over backwards. "Because you're a big shot billionaire. Get over yourself."

"As if dollar signs didn't appear in your eyes the second you realized who I am."

"Wow. We can add asshole to big shot."

If he thinks I care about his money, he is highly mistaken. Having money is a dealbreaker. Too bad. I wouldn't have minded a tumble in the sheets with his man. But I know better than to get involved with someone with money.

Chapter 5

"There's no such thing as peace. Not even in a billionaire's sauna."

JEREMY

I roll over in bed and check the time. Two a.m. and I'm wide awake. I blame the mountain of food I ate. And the pies. Oh, the pies.

Parker is a baking genius. The Rumrunner's Pecan Pie was dosed with dark spiced rum and brown sugar. I could have eaten the whole pie. Unfortunately, I had to fight off Eli's brothers to even get a slice. Eli wasn't kidding when he said his brothers are shit stirrers.

I don't understand why a woman with Parker's talents would waste them all on Smuggler's Hideaway. She could be running a bakery in New York City or a patisserie in Paris. And she seriously chooses this Podunk island?

I'm not getting back to sleep. I might as well get some work done.

I get comfortable in the sitting area in the corner of the room with my computer on my lap. I'd love a coffee, but I'm not disturbing the family by creeping downstairs to the kitchen.

"Wah!"

I nearly drop my laptop on the floor at the sound of Stephanie's crying. I wait until my pulse goes back to normal before returning my attention to my screen.

"Wah! Wah! Wah!"

I don't know if Stephanie is pissed or hungry or tired, but she's not quiet. I throw on a pair of shorts and a t-shirt before making my way downstairs. The second floor has all the bedrooms, while the first floor contains the living room, kitchen, and dining room. Surely, it'll be quiet down here.

I settle at the table in the dining room. It smells of lemon in here. I don't know how Paisley managed to clean up this room, considering the mess Eli's family made. I have never seen grown men get into a food fight before and I don't want to again.

Someone runs down the stairs before flinging open the kitchen door. I listen to drawers bang open and closed for a few minutes before I realize the dining room is not the refuge I was hoping it would be.

There's only one option left. I sneak down the stairs to the basement.

My penthouse in California is pretty impressive but this basement is in another world. There's a swimming pool, sauna, spa, and gym with more equipment than I've seen in some commercial fitness clubs.

"Wah!"

I groan. How is it possible to still hear the baby's cries in the basement? Stephanie has some serious lungs on her. Maybe she'll grow up to be an opera singer.

There's only one thing to do. I flip the lights on in the sauna before settling myself on the wooden bench. With the door closed, it's dead quiet. No babies crying. No doors slamming. Nothing.

It's bliss. I get to work.

Time ceases to exist as I work on the code for the app. The door opens some time later, but I ignore it.

Eli clears his throat.

"Just a minute," I mutter as I try to figure out this coding problem.

The laptop is snatched from my hands. "Hey! What are you doing?"

"Trust me. I'm saving you."

I frown. "Saving me?"

He checks his watch. "I expect my brothers and their partners and children to arrive any minute."

My brow wrinkles. "No one mentioned anything about swimming today at Thanksgiving yesterday."

"Probably because my brothers think they're clever and can sneak into my house."

"Don't you have security?"

"Anyway." He motions to the door. "You should get out of here before someone cranks on the heat without realizing you're in here."

"But this is the only quiet place in the house."

"Sorry. Stephanie has colic."

I blow out a breath. "No, I'm sorry. You kindly allowed me to stay here and I'm complaining about the noise. I'm an ungrateful guest."

"It's fine." He waves away my apology before sitting across from me. "Why are you working anyway? I thought you came to Smuggler's Hideaway for a break?"

"I did." I realize I'm scratching my neck and drop my hand. He raises an eyebrow.

"Fine. I haven't finished the coding on the Synq app yet."

He rears back. "What? Synq is launching at the start of the year."

"Yeah, I'm well aware."

"Why are you working on the coding? We have a whole team of developers." He holds up a hand before I can answer. "Never mind. I already know the answer. Mr. Control Freak strikes again."

"As if you're any better."

"At least I'm not hiding in your sauna trying to code when I should be enjoying a long weekend off work."

"It seemed logical when I came in here."

"Everything seems logical in the middle of the night." He stands. "Come on. Let's get some coffee and figure out a solution."

"There's nothing to figure out. I need to finish the coding. End of story."

He strolls out of the sauna and I chase after him. "Give me my laptop back."

"After you've eaten breakfast."

"Are you seriously holding my laptop hostage?"

"Wouldn't be the first time." He winks at me and I groan.

"Not fair. You can't bring up stuff that happened in college."

"Why not? It's fun."

"It wasn't fun when I had to beg Professor Nightly to let me re-take the final."

"You wouldn't have had to re-take the final if you hadn't locked me out of our dorm room."

"You did your chemistry experiment in the room. Do you know how long it took to get the smell out?"

We enter the kitchen and Eli strolls to the stove. "What do you want for breakfast?"

"I'm not hungry. I want to work."

"Too bad."

"Good morning," Paisley greets as she enters. I'm surprised she doesn't have a baby in her arms. "How did you sleep?"

"Someone," Eli points at me with the laptop, "was hiding in the sauna working."

"The sauna?" Paisley giggles. "You're lucky none of his brothers were around. They have declared the sauna a no clothes zone."

I shrug. "I can code naked as well as the next developer."

"But can you code naked when they're wiggling their naked asses in your face?"

My nose wrinkles. "Are you serious?"

She raises her eyebrows. "You met his brothers yesterday. Do you need to ask?"

No, I really don't.

"Why were you working in the sauna anyway? Is something wrong with your room? I swear, if the roof is leaking, I'm going to kill Flynn. I don't care if he's my best friend's fiancé. He's going down."

"The roof wasn't leaking. No need to go on a killing spree."

She blows out a breath. "Good. I don't want Stephanie to visit me in prison."

Eli wraps an arm around her shoulders. "As if you wouldn't manage to get away with murder."

"Can we maybe stop discussing ways to murder people now?" I ask.

"Okay." Paisley nods. "Back to why you couldn't work in your room. The roof doesn't leak. I know the bed is as comfortable as a cloud in heaven. What was the problem? Were you cold? And sought out the sauna for warmth?"

"I'm not used to having a baby in the house." A baby who can't stop screaming for hours on end.

Paisley sighs. "Sorry. She has colic."

"I wasn't complaining." Not out loud at least.

"I have an idea. But you probably won't like it." Her nose wrinkles before she sighs. "Forget I said anything."

"Paisley," Eli growls.

"What?" She bats her eyelashes at him.

"What are you up to?"

"Me?" She clutches her chest. "I'm trying to help out your friend, but I misspoke. I should have thought before I opened my mouth."

He narrows his eyes on her. "You always think before you open your mouth."

I clear my throat. "As much as I'm enjoying your weird nerdy foreplay, I am curious about Paisley's idea."

She grins at Eli in triumph. I nearly reconsider, but I can't hide in the sauna for the entire weekend. I'm okay with nudity but a bunch of men shoving their naked asses in my face? Not exactly a conducive environment to get this *Synq* app finished in.

"Parker has a loft above *Pirate's Pastries*. She rents it out to tourists during the summer but I believe it's empty at the moment."

Parker? I wouldn't mind spending more time with the beautiful woman. It's been a long time since I've been with a woman with her curves. Super models tend to be overly thin. They're boring to have dinner with, but they're usually up for just about anything between the sheets.

But I can't do anything right with Parker. First, she thought I was a reporter. And when she learned the truth – I'm a billionaire who could buy and sell her bakery a million times over – she appeared disgusted by me.

"I don't think Parker will rent to me."

"Parker can't be picky," Eli mutters.

"What do you mean?" Is Parker in money trouble? I don't understand how. She must have delivered over a hundred pies yesterday. And based on what Eli and Paisley paid, they weren't cheap either.

Paisley elbows Eli. "Ignore him. He has a big mouth. What do you say? Shall I contact Parker?"

"Nah. I'll drive over there. I want a look at the place before I commit."

Besides, I don't want to give Parker the chance to say no. If I'm there in person and she truly does need money, she'll have a harder time denying me in person.

My hands tingle and my pulse quickens as excitement flows through me at the idea of seeing the baker again. My body doesn't care how she hates me.

I agree. She'll change her mind about me once she gets to know me.

And then… Well, then, maybe we can have some fun before I leave this island for good.

Chapter 6

"Nothing burns faster than cookies... except boundaries."

PARKER

Bake the pies with rum and sugar,
Fa la la la la, la la, yarrrr.
Stir 'til pirates start to stagger,
Fa la la la la, la la, yarrrr.
Roll the crust with flair and flourish,

I sing at the top of my voice as I spoon the dough for the Kelpie Crunch cookies onto a baking sheet and shove it in the oven.

I set the timer since I have no desire to scrape burned cookies from my baking sheet this morning. And even less desire to deal with the fire department. Although, I wasn't joking about how cute the new firefighter is. Not as sexy as a certain billionaire, though.

Jeremy. Now there's a sexy man I wouldn't mind watching run into my bakery. Preferably without a shirt on. With his hair all messy and his light brown eyes focused on me.

Phew. It's getting hot in here.

Too bad Jeremy's a billionaire. Men with money are off limits with a capital O and a hell to the no. I've learned my lesson there and I don't need a repeat.

I shove all thoughts of men and their treachery away and gather the ingredients for my baked peaches and cream whiskey muffins. I sing as I get to work.

Roll the crust with flair and flourish,
Hide the moonshine, don't be slow!
If the smugglers start to scurry,
Feed them pie, then out they go!

"What are you singing?" a man asks from behind me.

I scream and grab a weapon as I whirl around to confront him.

Jeremy chuckles. "What are you going to do with a pastry brush? Brush me with butter?"

I frown at the pastry brush. I thought I'd grabbed my rolling pin. A rolling pin can do some damage. Trust me. You don't want a rolling pin to the skull.

"What in the name of Kraken are you doing in here?"

He lifts a brow. "Kraken?"

"Do you not know what a Kraken is? Gigantic tentacled beast feared for its ability to engulf entire ships and cause deadly whirlwinds?"

"I wasn't expecting to be compared to a mythical sea creature this morning."

I start to explain how Krakens aren't mythical but then I realize I have more important questions. "Why are you in my kitchen? What makes you think you can just waltz right inside here?"

Typical billionaire behavior. They think they can do whatever they want because they have money. News flash. Not everyone is impressed with money.

"Sorry. I did knock but you must not have heard me." He pauses but when I don't admit to being too loud to hear a knock, he continues, "I tried the door and it was unlocked."

"And you thought, 'Hey! A woman working alone in her kitchen won't mind if a strange man shows up'."

"I'm not a strange man. We've met before. I'm Eli's friend."

I could tell him how most women are murdered by men they know but let's face it, facts won't make a difference to this man.

"What do you want?" I check the time. "At six in the morning."

He flinches a bit at my comment on time. Shocker. Does the billionaire actually have a conscious?

"I …um…" He stuffs his hands in his pockets. "Heard you have a loft for rent."

"I seriously doubt my loft is good enough for a billionaire to stay in."

He shrugs. "As long as there are no babies around, I'm good."

I purse my lips. "What kind of man hates babies?"

"I don't hate babies."

I snort. "And I don't love chocolate and have the hips to prove it."

His gaze dips to my hips and his eyes flare. Whoa. Flare? My chronic lack of sleep must be causing hallucinations. No way billionaire Jeremy's eyes flared when he looked at my hips.

He blows out a breath. "Seriously. I don't hate babies. But I do need to work and Stephanie has colic."

I motion toward the mess in the kitchen. "I doubt I'm any quieter than Stephanie."

"As long as you're not baking at 2 a.m., we won't have a problem."

"I have been known to bake at 2 a.m. before."

He flicks a hand in dismissal. "Baking won't bother me."

Screw the smugglers! Can't he buy a hint?

"I only rent by the month in the off-season." It's a lie, but the idea of having this man who my hormones want to throw a party for in close proximity is a bit more than my poor brain can handle.

"A month sounds good. In fact, let's say until the end of the year."

"I thought you were only visiting for the weekend."

He smirks. "Paying attention to how long I'm staying?"

More like when he's leaving.

"You haven't seen the place yet. It won't meet your billion-aire standards."

He rubs his hands together. "Let's see this place then."

I try to think of another reason why he won't want the place but I'm all out. "Fine," I mumble and grab the keys from a hook near the door. "Let's go."

"There's a private entrance," I explain as I go outside.

I unlock the door to the apartment and motion him forward but he doesn't move. "After you."

Awesome. He's going to stare at my jiggly butt the whole time. I try to control how much it jiggles but give up and end up running up the stairs instead.

"This door has another lock on it," I explain as I unlock the second door.

I step inside the loft. "This is it. It's only one room, but you have everything you need. Kitchen, bathroom, living room, sleeping alcove."

I stop speaking when I realize Jeremy isn't listening. He's wandering around the space, touching everything.

"Is there Wi-Fi?" he asks as he opens the bathroom door to inspect inside.

"Wi-Fi and you have all the streaming channels you could dream of on the television." The booking agency I use to rent out the loft during the summer insisted on it. I tried explaining how no one who visits the island of Smuggler's Hideaway watches television, but they wouldn't listen.

"Good." He exits the bathroom and stalks toward me. "I'll take it." He holds out his hand for the keys.

"I'll need you to pay for the month in advance and I also require a five-hundred-dollar security deposit in case of any damage."

"Will you accept a check?"

I chew on my bottom lip as I consider it. I don't usually accept checks. But this is Eli's friend and a billionaire. I should probably make an exception.

"Never mind," he grumbles and I whip my head up to meet his gaze. Except his gaze isn't on my eyes. It's on my lip. And his light brown eyes have darkened with passion. With passion?

Get ahold of yourself, Parker Shaw. No billionaire is interested in a chubby baker living in a small town on a small island.

"Check's fine," I squeak.

He grins. "It's okay. You don't have to make an exception for me." He whips out his phone. "I'll transfer the money now."

"You don't even know how much it is yet."

"It'll be fine."

Thanks for reminding me you have money to burn. The alarm on my phone goes off. Speaking of burning.

"My cookies!" I rush down the stairs toward the kitchen.

Jeremy chases after me. "Slow down! You're going to break your neck."

I ignore him as I reach the bottom of the stairs and fly out the door. My apron catches on the latch and I'm flung backwards. Straight into Jeremy's arms.

"You need to be careful," he growls.

My skin tingles where he touches me. I wonder how it would feel if he touched other areas of skin. Would it tingle, too? My breath catches as I imagine his fingers kneading my breasts. I moan.

"Are you okay? Did you hurt yourself?"

My cheeks heat as embarrassment hits me. "I'm fine," I croak.

His brow wrinkles. "You're flushed. Maybe—"

My alarm chimes again. My cookies! I push away from him and run toward the kitchen. I fling the door open and rush to the oven. I remember to grab a towel at the last second before removing the cookies.

I place the baking sheet on the prep table before studying the cookies.

"They aren't burnt. Good. I hate the smell of burnt cookies."

Jeremy chuckles and I startle. I forgot all about him in my haste to get to my cookies.

"Burn cookies often?"

"Only when I'm distracted by someone desperate for a place to stay because he's afraid of a little baby."

He scowls. "Send me an invoice."

He stomps off. Once the door is closed behind him, I slump against the table. Too close for comfort. Another second in Jeremy's arms and I would have forgotten all about his wealth and begged him to carry me upstairs and have his wicked way with me.

Not happening. This woman does not get involved with billionaires. Not anymore, at least.

Chapter 7

"Note to self: never touch a woman's piping bag without permission."

JEREMY

I yawn as I settle at the dining room table to get some work done. I slept surprisingly well, but not nearly long enough, judging by how the lights on the main street in Smuggler's Rest aren't on yet.

While my computer warms up, I glance around Parker's loft. I have to admit it's cute. Small but thoughtfully done. Despite being one room, it doesn't feel cramped.

There are exposed beams overhead, polished smooth and stained the color of driftwood. The kitchen gleams with copper accents and sea-glass cabinet knobs. A ship's wheel – repurposed as a quirky towel rack – hangs on one wall.

Everything is crisp and clean with throw pillows in mermaid-scale patterns. The craftsmanship is solid – real wood, real stone, not the fake mass-produced crap you usually find in overpriced rentals. This place says: *someone built this with their hands. And someone weirder decorated it.*

As I work, the scent of vanilla and cinnamon grows stronger. Parker must be baking. Say I'm a caveman but I love the idea of working on my computer while my woman bakes in the kitchen.

Except Parker isn't my woman and – judging by the hate spitting from her eyes whenever she glances my way – she never will be.

Which is good. I don't want a woman. They can't be trusted. Especially when they get a look at my bank account. And who has time for one anyway? Short affairs with women whose names I can barely remember is the way to go.

There's a crash downstairs and I startle. Shit. My fingers slipped on the keyboard. Where was I? I scan through the lines of code in an effort to figure it out.

But then there's another crash.

Damnit. I'm never going to figure out what I did with this racket going on. What is Parker doing downstairs? Pounding cookies into submission? Baking shouldn't be this loud.

I slam my laptop shut and tromp down the stairs. I knock on the door to the bakery, but I don't wait for her to respond before entering.

"What are you…." I pause when I realize Parker is decorating a cake. And I don't mean decorating in the way Mom used to. This cake is amazing. There's a mermaid, a treasure chest, and what appears to be a pirate.

Parker finishes the mermaid's tail before glancing up at me. "What do you want?"

"I heard some loud bangs."

"Wasn't me." She motions to the cake. "I've been too busy to bang around the kitchen."

"Sorry. I didn't mean to disturb you."

She sets the piping bag on the table before stretching out her wrist and wiggling her fingers.

"Are you hurt?"

"Fine. Just cramping from working on this monster of a cake all morning."

I don't hesitate. I grasp her hand and begin to massage her fingers. She moans and my cock twitches. It wants to hear her moan while I'm massaging other parts of her body. Its vote is for her breasts, but it wouldn't mind her ass either.

Her eyes close and her head falls back, exposing her neck I want to nibble on. My cock is on board with this plan.

"I should hire you to massage my hand after every cake decorating session."

I grunt. "Sorry, darling, you can't afford me."

She snatches her hand away. "Thanks for the reminder, Mr. Moneybags."

My cock deflates and I sigh. "I was joking."

"Joking about money isn't funny," she snarls.

"Sorry. Sometimes I forget…."

"Forget what?" she asks when I trail off. "That not everyone in the world is made of money? That money doesn't actually grow on trees? Pray tell. What do you forget?"

I run a hand through my hair. "All of the above?"

"Whatever. If you want coffee, grab yourself a cup from the machine. It's easy to use. An idiot could figure it out."

I get the hint. I'm the idiot.

"Thanks. I could use some coffee." I start toward the café but then there's another loud bang. "What is happening outside?"

I don't wait for her answer before heading out the back door. Parker follows me. I search the area for the cause of the noise. There's a truck with a ladder rack parked in the middle of the street.

"What is the truck doing?"

Parker sighs. "I love this time of year."

She hasn't cleared up my confusion one bit.

She smiles up at me. "They're hanging up the Christmas lights and decorations."

"Now? It's past Thanksgiving."

"Which is the whole point." I must appear confused – I am confused – since she explains. "The businesses of Smuggler's Hideaway have an agreement. No Christmas decorations until after Thanksgiving."

"Meanwhile, the rest of the world has been buying Christmas candy since before Halloween."

Her nose wrinkles. It's adorable. I want to kiss it. "I doubt every single country in the world has been eating Christmas candy since Halloween."

"Nah. Just the civilized ones."

She crosses her arms over her chest and I try not to look but my eyes slip and I get a glimpse of her cleavage. It's magnificent. I fear I'm going to be spending a lot of time fantasizing about it while in her bed above her bakery.

"I forgot you think Smuggler's Hideaway is Podunk central."

I cringe. I never should have used the word Podunk. In my defense, I was lost and annoyed at being sent on a wild goose chase.

"What kind of Christmas decorations do they put up? Mermaids? Pirates?"

"Are you making fun of the decorations in the loft? You can go stay at the Mermaid Hotel instead. They haven't renovated in thirty years but you won't have to deal with quirky decorations."

I was joking again. But I know better than to admit to it. Someone is a bit prickly.

A man jumps out of the truck and Parker waves to him. "Hey, Flynn."

He grins as he saunters toward us. "Parker, my baking queen, your Pearl Diver Pie was delicious as usual."

He hugs her and I bite back a growl. He shouldn't be touching her.

What the hell? I don't do jealousy. And certainly not over a small-town baker. But the fire in my belly calls me a liar.

"Who's this?" I ask and they pull apart.

"Flynn, Jeremy. Jeremy, Flynn. Flynn is the local contractor and all-around handyman. Jeremy is staying in the loft above the bakery."

I'm surprised Parker didn't mention I'm a billionaire. Most women can't wait to share the information as if they're special by association to me. Maybe she isn't like most women?

Flynn offers me his hand and he squeezes mine as we shake. He thinks he can scare me away from Parker? He has another thing coming.

I squeeze his hand harder in return. We stare at each other as we each try to squeeze the other's hand as hard as possible. My bones crack, but I don't give up.

Parker pushes her way in between us. "What is wrong with you two? Why don't you whip out your dicks and I can measure them?"

Flynn smirks. "Sophia might kill me if you come near my dick."

Parker rolls her eyes. "Sophia would totally understand when I explain the context."

Flynn smiles. "Yeah, my girl would."

His girl? Is Parker not his girl? Is he cheating on Parker? Or the other way around?

I blow out a breath. This is not me. I don't get jealous. I'm not possessive. Besides, Flynn did say Sophia wouldn't want Parker around his dick. They're not involved. I need to calm down.

"What are you up to?" Parker asks Flynn.

"Getting the Christmas decorations and the lights up." Flynn frowns. "But my crew abandoned me."

"Abandoned you?"

"A few too many drinks at *Bootlegger* last night."

Parker giggles. "At least it's not Mermaid Karaoke season."

"Mermaid Karaoke?" I ask.

She waves away my question. "It's a tourist thing in the summer. You'll be long gone by then."

She can't wait to get rid of me. I wish the feeling was mutual.

"Hey! You're an engineer, aren't you?" she asks.

"A software engineer."

"But you know about electricity and all that stuff."

"All that stuff?"

"This is a good idea," Flynn says.

I glance back and forth between them. "What idea? I didn't hear an idea."

"You can help Flynn with the decorations," Parker declares.

"I need to finish my coding work."

She lifts an eyebrow. "The same work you couldn't concentrate on because you heard a few little thumps outside?"

"Yes."

She shoves me toward Flynn. "Help him. It'll clear your mind. And give you more energy than coffee."

"Doing manual labor will give me energy?"

Her response? She waves as she returns to the bakery.

Flynn laughs beside me and I scowl at him. "I wasn't laughing at you, but you have to admit Parker totally conned you."

She didn't con me. I let her con me. Because she's right. I am having a hard time concentrating on my work. And I could use a break. How did she know? She notices entirely too much about me.

Chapter 8

"I should've brought rum instead of coffee."

PARKER

I reach the entrance to town hall and swear under my breath. My hands are full since I'm carrying a tray of cookies and a tray of coffee.

"I need more hands," I mutter as I try stacking the trays.

"I got it." Jeremy opens the door for me while simultaneously rescuing the tray of coffee.

"Thank you." The billionaire might annoy me, but I can be polite.

"You're welcome."

Okay. I'm calling it. It is totally unfair Jeremy is a billionaire who also has a sexy, deep voice to match his handsome face. He couldn't be a troll I can ignore? Rude.

I wiggle my hand. "I can take the tray back now."

"I'll carry it."

I purse my lips. "Don't you have somewhere you need to be? Money to burn? Code to write? People to fire?"

He raises a brow. "Money to burn?"

I shrug. "While doing an evil laugh."

He chuckles. "I guess I need to practice my evil laugh." He clears his throat. "I'm meeting Eli."

"Here? In city hall?"

"He told me to meet him at the meeting room in city hall."

"Impossible."

"Is there no meeting room?"

"No, there is a meeting room. But the meeting room is booked for a meeting about the *Mermaid Treasure Hunt.*"

His brow wrinkles. "*Mermaid Treasure Hunt?*"

"It's one of my favorite holiday events. Participants are given a treasure map with clues of where gifts are hidden around the island. Whoever manages to collect the most gifts wins. And, because this is Smuggler's Hideaway, you have to drink a shot of moonshine every time you find a gift. Which is why the treasure hunt is conducted on bikes."

"And you're helping to organize the event?"

I can't stop the smile from spreading on my face. "I'm hoping *Pirate's Pastries* will be chosen as a location on the treasure map."

"You've never been a stop before?"

I lift my free hand and cross my fingers. "Maybe this year is my year."

He smiles at me and my breath catches. He has two dimples – one on each cheek – to match the dimple on his chin. He went from sexy to panty-melting-sexy with a smile.

"You've got this, Parker. Your bakery is fabulous. Smuggler's Hideaway would be stupid not to include you."

"Thanks." Ugh! I sound breathless.

I am not allowed to go all breathless for a billionaire who cares more about money and getting what he wants than other people. I clear my throat.

"Anyway, you can't be meeting Eli in the meeting room since the committee already reserved the room."

We reach the meeting room and my heart thumps in my chest.

Being a stop on the treasure hunt would expose the bakery to a ton of new tourists. More than half of the tourists to the island are repeat visitors. All I need is one chance to show them my baked goods and coffee is just as good – if not better – than the chain coffee place on the boardwalk.

My hand shakes as I reach for the door. Jeremy nudges me out of the way. "I'll get the door."

"Since when are you a gentleman?"

"I'm not." He winks as he ushers me into the room.

I slow to a halt when I notice the room is empty except for Lana, the mayor, and Jennifer, the town secretary.

"Am I early?"

Lana motions to a chair across from her. "No, dear, you're right on time."

"And you brought goodies," Jennifer cheers.

I set the tray of cookies on their table while Jeremy hands out the coffee.

Lana licks her lips as she rakes her gaze over Jeremy. "Extra points for bringing man candy."

My cheeks warm and I sputter, "Oh, I didn't… He's not…"

"I'm meeting Eli here later," Jeremy finishes for me when I run out of steam.

Jennifer flips through her agenda. "I don't have Eli in my diary."

Jeremy frowns. "He messaged me to meet him here at this time."

"Today?" she asks.

"Yes. Today."

Lana winks at him. "I, for one, don't mind if he stays for the interview."

"Interview?" My brow wrinkles. "What interview? I thought this was a meeting of the committee for the *Mermaid Treasure Hunt*."

"Have a seat, dear, and I'll explain."

I sit on the chair Lana indicates. When I'm seated, I scan the room and realize it's set up for interviews. Lana and Jennifer are sitting at a large table at the front of the room and there's one chair in the middle, which I'm sitting on. The rest of the chairs are pushed to the back wall.

Great glistening krakens. This is an interview. I thought I was a shoo-in.

"I'll just…" Jeremy sits in the back of the room and digs out his phone.

Great. The billionaire is going to sit there and watch my interview? As if this isn't nerve wracking enough, a man who has hit it out of the park with his business is going to watch me fight for the survival of my bakery. Awesome. Just awesome.

"Shall we get started?" Lana asks. I nod and she continues, "There are ten stops on the treasure map each year. We try to vary the stops to keep tourists coming back every year."

"*Pirate's Pastries* has never been a stop before, but I'd love to participate."

"As you know, participants who manage to figure out your location and find the gift hidden there are required to drink a shot of moonshine. As a stop on the treasure hunt, you're also a sponsor of the event, which means we expect you to pay for the gift and the moonshine."

I swallow. The gift *and* the moonshine? "I assume I can bake a gift. I figured I'd bake a cookie to match the clue used to find my location. I can make pirate-shaped cookies or little mermaid cupcakes. As long as I know the clue in advance, I can design an appropriate gift."

Jennifer moans. "As long as the gift tastes as good as your Siren's Snaps, your stop will be a hit."

"And we have an agreement with *Buccaneer's Whiskey* for you to buy the moonshine from them," Lana adds.

"How much moonshine are we talking about?"

"We usually have about five thousand participants in the treasure hunt."

I clasp my chest. "I need to buy enough moonshine for five thousand people?"

The mayor waves a hand in dismissal. "At least a quarter of the participants drop out early."

"Which leaves nearly four thousand people for me to buy moonshine for."

My stomach plummets. I can't afford to buy moonshine for four hundred people, let alone four thousand. So much for participating in the *Mermaid Treasure Hunt* and growing my client base.

I stand. "I'm afraid I'll have to withdraw my application to participate in the treasure hunt."

"Oh dear," Lana mutters. "This happens every year."

Jeremy clears his throat. "Actually, *Apparoo* would be happy to sponsor the treasure hunt by providing the moonshine for all of the stops."

I glance over my shoulder to glare at him. "I don't need your help."

"I didn't say you did."

"No, you just happened to have a meeting with Eli at the same time as my interview *and* when I withdraw my application, you happen to remember you were planning to sponsor the event."

"Yes?"

I roll my eyes. "How stupid do you think people are on this Podunk island?"

He scratches the back of his neck. "I'm sorry. I never should have referred to Smuggler's Hideaway as a Podunk island. It was rude and judgmental."

"Whatever. It doesn't matter. I don't need some billionaire coming to my rescue."

"Hold on," Lana says before Jeremy can respond. "The town of Smuggler's Rest would like to accept his offer to sponsor the event."

"Go ahead. This no longer involves me."

"Don't be stupid, Parker."

I spin around to face Jeremy. "Do not call me stupid."

"Stop being stubborn."

My eyes widen. "And now I'm stubborn. Wow. You really know how to compliment a woman."

"If you'd calm down for a minute, you'd realize this is a great opportunity for the bakery."

"I didn't realize there was going to be a show this morning," Lana mutters. "We should have brought popcorn."

"Popcorn? Who needs popcorn? We have cookies." Jennifer slides the tray of cookies across the table to Lana.

Great. My little spat with Jeremy is going to be all over the island before lunchtime. The residents of Smuggler's Hideaway do love their gossip. I usually stay out of it. I'm too busy trying to save my bakery to care about gossip.

I march to the table and grab the tray of leftover coffee. "Feel free to finish the cookies. But please return my tray to the bakery."

I continue toward the door.

"You're going to run away?" Jeremy taunts.

I spin around so I can properly fire the lasers in my eyes at him. Jeremy Holland is a complete and total jerk. I can't believe I was softening to the billionaire. I know better!

"I'm not running away. I'm leaving this meeting as I am no longer involved in the treasure hunt."

He crosses his arms over his chest and I ignore the way his biceps bulge with the motion. Yep. I'll be ignoring those muscles starting in a few seconds. Just as soon as my eyes listen to my brain's instructions. Any second now.

"Liar. You're running away because you don't want my help since you have a problem with me."

"Wrong. I don't want your help because I don't need some billionaire to waltz onto this island and save me like I'm some dimwitted woman who can't handle life herself."

I don't give him the chance to respond before I throw the door open and stomp away.

Stupid billionaires sticking their noses where they don't belong. Why was he even in the meeting? No way did Eli arrange a meeting in the town hall for this morning.

Whatever. I don't care. I'm staying away from Jeremy from now on. I can ignore how he lives above my bakery. I won't wonder what he's doing while I'm downstairs baking. Nope. Not I.

Chapter 9

"I came for coffee. I stayed for the woman wielding a piping bag like a weapon."

JEREMY

I growl at my computer. Why is this code not working? Crap. I'm going to have to go back to the beginning and check every single line.

And I will. But first. Coffee.

I stand and rub my eyes as I make my way to the kitchen for another cup of coffee. I pick up the container of coffee cups. Crap. It's empty.

Desperate for caffeine, I check the refrigerator. Maybe there's a Coke in here. Except it's empty. Probably because I haven't done any grocery shopping since I arrived in town. I've been relying on the coffee and basket of food Parker provided with the rental.

I grab my phone and walk to the door. There's no better time than the present to get some shopping done. Except when I'm outside, I realize it's still the middle of the night. The grocery store won't be open yet.

ᴧere is a light on in the bakery. And Parker's coffee is ᴧcellent.

Too bad she'll probably skin me alive with her cake knife after our last conversation. I didn't mean to upset her. I thought providing for the moonshine would help her out. She obviously didn't want to front the money for the alcohol.

Instead of thanking me, she threw my offer back at me and tried to kill me with those daggers in her eyes. The woman is the most prickly, the most stubborn, the most gorgeous woman I've ever met.

She's also my one chance for coffee at this time of morning. I knock on the back door of the kitchen.

"Come in," she shouts. I enter and she frowns at me. "What are you doing here? I figured you'd be long gone from Smuggler's Hideaway by now."

I'd planned to be gone. Spend Thanksgiving weekend with Eli and his family. Get a break from coding. And return to work on the *Synq* app with a fresh mind.

Unfortunately, I'm as stuck on the coding as I was when I arrived. I'm not going anywhere until this app is finished.

I shrug. "I paid for the apartment until the new year. I figured I might as well use it."

She snorts. "As if the money you paid can even make a dent in your bank account."

"Hey. It makes a dent." She lifts an eyebrow. "A very small dent."

She shakes her head. "What are you doing here at this time of the morning?"

"I couldn't…" I break off to yawn.

"Maybe you should go back to bed."

"No can do. I need to work."

She nods to the café. "Go ahead and make yourself a coffee."

I don't hesitate. While I'm at it, I go ahead and make a coffee for her as well. I assume she drinks it black since there was no sugar or creamer in the loft.

"Here you go." I set the coffee down on the table in front of her.

She groans. "Thank Neptune. I could use a caffeine jolt."

"What are you working on?"

"A gingerbread house."

I scan the kitchen and notice there are parts of a gingerbread house – walls, roof tiles, chimneys, etc. – everywhere. "How big will it be?"

She giggles. "Huge."

"What are you doing with a huge gingerbread house?"

"It's for the gingerbread contest. The winner's prize is ten thousand dollars and a contract to supply baked goods to city hall for the year."

Based on the meeting the other day at city hall, Parker could use the money. "I bet you win."

"Not if I don't finish assembling this gingerbread house. Between the assembly, setting, and decorating, I don't know if I'm going to finish in time. The entries have to be at city hall by ten this morning."

She glances at the clock on the wall and her eyes widen as she nibbles on her bottom lip. My cock twitches. It wants to feel those plump lips surrounding it.

Knock it off, I order my body. Parker's seriously worried about this and she needs the money.

"How can I help?"

She blinks up at me. "Help? You want to help?"

"I am an engineer."

She snorts. "I thought *software* engineers didn't know how to assemble things."

I scowl. I'm not doing great at being a software engineer at the moment – the *Synq* app is a great example of my failures – but I'm not going to whine and complain to Parker about my work.

"I can take direction."

"Seriously?" Her eyes widen. "A man who can take direction? Are you certain you're not a merman?"

"What the hell is a merman?" I tease. I know what a merman is, but I love to watch Parker get all worked up. The woman is serious about her sea lore.

She huffs. "Don't let anyone else on Smuggler's Hideaway find out you have no idea what the male equivalent of a mermaid is."

"I have legs and not the tail of a fish. Pretty sure I'm not a merman." I kick out a leg before circling it around. "See. All legs."

Her eyes flare as she stares at me. Little Miss Prickly is interested. She doesn't want to be, but she is.

She clears her throat. "You can hold the walls while I pipe the icing to glue the pieces together." She whirls around and gathers several wall pieces before placing them on the thick cardboard tray decorated with holiday-themed paper.

"Hold these two together." She arranges two walls at an angle. My fingers brush hers as I take over for her and a jolt of electricity hits me. Judging by how Parker jumped away from me, she felt it as well. Interesting.

She grabs the piping bag and leans over to glue the sides together. Her shirt gapes open and I catch a glimpse of her breasts fighting to be contained by her bra.

My fingers itch to touch her. To explore her skin. Will a jolt of electricity hit me if I did?

"Hold still," she growls and I realize my hands are actually shaking.

"My hands are cramping," I lie, since I'm not telling this woman who hates me how I can't stop thinking about touching her. Her cake knife is way too close for that conversation to happen.

"It's been a whole thirty seconds. Don't be a wimp."

"I'll have you know I work out every day."

"In which case, you should have better stamina."

"I have stamina," I grumble.

I'm not referring to working out. Judging by the blush spreading over her cheeks, she knows exactly what I'm referring to. My cock twitches. Again. It seems to do a lot of twitching whenever Parker is around. Especially considering how much the woman hates me.

"This side is done," she finally says in a breathy voice, which is doing nothing to help my cock calm down. "Grab the wall there." She nods toward another piece of the gingerbread house.

We work together in silence for the next twenty minutes to assemble the rest of the walls and roof panels.

"There." She drops the piping bag on the table.

"We're finished?"

She chortles. "Finished? Not hardly. It needs to set for an hour before I can add the windows, doors, and other decorations."

"Coffee?"

"Don't you need to get back to work?"

I do, but I wasn't getting anything accomplished anyway. "Nah. I have time."

We settle at a table in the corner of the café with our drinks. Parker closes her eyes and moans as she sips on her coffee. I notice she has bruises beneath her eyes, and her face is pale. She's exhausted.

"You need rest."

"Ha! What I need is to stop changing my mind about the design of the gingerbread house."

"Is changing your mind why you're on a time crunch?"

"I kept second-guessing everything. I had a whole plan and then decided I hated it halfway through."

"Ah. The classic artist spiral. Right before the masterpiece."

"Masterpiece? If by masterpiece you mean a slightly lopsided gingerbread house held together with desperation and royal icing, sure."

There's a long pause. The café is quiet. The only noise is the hum of the coffee machine. I study her face. Her ponytail is starting to come loose, and a dusting of flour clings to the tips of her bangs.

I reach over without thinking and tuck a strand of hair behind her ear.

She freezes. Her eyes flick up to mine.

"Flour," I mumble, drawing my hand back. "You had some."

"Thanks."

"Want help?"

"With what? Designing gumdrop shutters or deciding if a sour belt can be a doormat?"

"I'm excellent with candy-based architectural dilemmas."

"I couldn't let you. You came downstairs in the middle of the night because you needed coffee to fuel your work, and in the meantime, I've stolen you away."

"I'll get back to work after the gingerbread house is finished."

"Fine. You can help. But if the roof caves in because you breathe wrong, I'm blaming you."

"Deal," I say, lifting my cup in salute. "But if we win, I'm taking full credit."

"In your dreams, Holland."

But her smile lingers as she stands to check the gingerbread structure.

And that might be the sweetest part of the morning.

Chapter 10

"I came to slay with sugar, not get ambushed by guilt."

PARKER

I roll the gingerbread house into city hall at five minutes to ten. With Jeremy's help, I was able to finish decorating the house, including adding all the candy waves, sugar pearls, and fondant mermaids on time.

Although, I did have to stop him from trying to pipe icing when a large blob exploded from his piping bag. Good thing the blob landed on his shoes and not on my gingerbread house.

I giggle at the memory. Who thought Jeremy, the billionaire who thinks Smuggler's Hideaway is a Podunk island, would help out at my bakery? I never expected a billionaire to have blue icing on his shoe. Maybe he's not as much of an asshole as I thought.

I reach the foyer. "I'm here!"

The area is a hive of activity. There are at least twenty bakers setting up their gingerbread houses. My stomach drops. I didn't think there would be this many entries.

Son of a barnacle. I knew I should have protested when the city council opened the contest to non-inhabitants of the island.

Lana and Jennifer make their way toward me. "We were worried you wouldn't make the deadline," Jennifer says.

She's not the only one.

Lana frowns. "I wasn't worried. I knew you'd be here."

"Where do you want me?"

There are tables scattered around the foyer to display the gingerbread houses to visitors who can vote on their favorite house. The house with the most votes wins. I'm hoping my Smuggler's Hideaway themed gingerbread house will be a local favorite.

"We have your table right here." Lana motions to a table in the middle of the foyer.

I want to cry. This location is the best one. Not only is it in the middle of the room, but the table is the largest and it's slightly elevated. No one entering city hall will fail to notice it.

"Chop. Chop," Jennifer says. "You've met the ten o'clock deadline, but you still need to have your gingerbread house in place with any extra decorations by noon."

I nod to them before slowly rolling my creation through the room to my spot. As I pass the other gingerbread houses, I evaluate them. All of them appear perfect but they're also boring. Not a mermaid or pirate or kraken amongst them.

Smuggler's Hideaway doesn't enjoy boring. Good. Maybe I can win this contest after all.

I begin by placing a treasure map table runner with "X marks the spot" near where the house itself will be. I ordered this table runner when I thought *Pirate's Pastries* was going to be included in the *Mermaid Treasure Hunt.*

My stomach sours. The treasure hunt was a great opportunity to expand my business and save my bakery from bankruptcy. Next year, I promise myself. Next year I'll have the cash to be a stop on the hunt.

With as much caution as possible, I transfer my gingerbread house to the table. Once it's in place and hasn't broken, I can breathe again.

Okay. Time to get to work. For the next two hours, I scatter chocolate gold coins and rock candy 'crystals' around the house. I add mini fondant moonshine barrels and tiny candy rum bottles, as well as gingerbread pirate figures. I coil licorice ropes around the pirate figures before adding gummy fish, starfish, and jelly sea creatures.

And now for the finishing touch. I use icing to create kraken tentacles that peek out from underneath the house and add edible glitter to give the entire display a magical sea sparkle.

When I'm finished, I step back to admire my creation. It's perfect. It's a bit eccentric with the pirates and sea creatures, but this is Smuggler's Hideaway, where we believe in mermaids. Eccentric is part of our charm.

"Time!" Lana yells. "From this point forward, you are not allowed to touch your gingerbread house. Jennifer will photograph each house every morning to ensure no one's cheating."

Smugglers love to cheat, but since there aren't any other locals entered in the contest, I'm not worried about anyone cheating.

I pack up my supplies and place them on my cart. Jennifer arrives and snaps a picture of the house.

"I knew your gingerbread house would be awesome," she says as she tapes the picture to the corner of the table.

"Of course, it's awesome. Parker attended one of the best pastry schools in the country."

"The best? I think you mean the most expensive."

Flipping fishcakes. What are my parents doing here?

Jennifer pats my arm. She's well aware of the relationship I have with my parents. Everyone on the island is. It's impossible to keep a secret here, especially when you decide to move out of your parents' house in the middle of the night.

"I'm okay," I whisper to her.

She purses her lips. She doesn't believe me, but she moves on to photograph the next gingerbread house. Thank the mermaids. The town secretary is the queen of the gossiping inhabitants. The last thing I need is for her to eavesdrop on my conversation.

I blow out a breath and force myself to turn around to face my parents.

"Mom, Dad. How are you doing?"

Mom scowls at me. "You'd know if you'd bothered to show up to our house for Thanksgiving."

Bothered to show up? They never invited me.

"I was working all day on Thanksgiving."

"You must have missed our house when you were out delivering pies," Dad says.

I fist my hands. This is what they mean by 'show up'. Not show up to spend the holiday meal with them. Nope. 'Show up' as in give them a pie free of charge.

I'm supposed to supply their baking needs and yet they complain about my business not doing well. Do they not understand the correlation between the two?

"I thought you went to *Hideaway Haven Resort* for Thanksgiving."

Hideaway Haven Resort is an exclusive and super fancy hotel and restaurant on the beach. Hudson Clark built the place after he got injured and was forced to retire from the NFL.

My parents spend all of their holidays at the resort because they can afford it. While they complain about how expensive my culinary school education was, they don't need the money. They're orthodontists and have the sole orthodontic practice on the island.

My dad's nose wrinkles. "Their pumpkin pie was very bland this year."

"I spoke to Hudson," Mom says and I bite my tongue before I groan. I also try to come up with another topic of conversation. But I don't manage before she speaks again. "He's searching for a new pastry chef."

I'm aware since he contacted me and offered me the job. But I'm not closing my bakery to work for someone else. I don't do well under someone else's control. Witness my interactions with my parents.

"I'm certain he'll find someone," I say.

"You could go work for him," she pushes and I sigh. Here we go.

"He pays very well," Dad adds.

My parents don't care how much the job pays. They care that the resort is owned by a famous man and, therefore, is prestigious. Unlike owning a quirky little bakery.

"Did you ask him what the salary is?" I can't stop myself from poking at my parents. Money isn't everything but try and tell them anything of the kind.

Dad's eyes light up. "You're interested?" He digs out his phone. "I bet Hudson would interview you today."

"I'm not interested. I have a business to run."

Dad shoves his phone back in his pocket. "A business to run into the ground," he mutters just loud enough for me to hear.

"Things are going well. Thanks for asking."

I'm not lying. Much. Thanksgiving was a success and once I win this gingerbread house contest, I'll have ten thousand dollars to put toward my debts. Plus, the loft above the bakery is rented out for two months when it usually sits empty.

Things aren't all doom and gloom for *Pirate's Pastries.*

"Going well?" Mom raises her eyebrows at me. I don't squirm. She can't guilt me. She lost the right after all of the snide comments.

Why aren't you running a patisserie in Paris? Why did you return to this island? You're such a disappointment. I thought you had grand ideas.

I did have grand ideas. Which were crushed by one asshole who I never told my parents about. I knew exactly how they'd react and I had no interest in being caught up in litigation for years. No thanks.

I force a smile. "Yes, going well."

"The chain coffee place on the boardwalk is packed whenever I'm there," Dad says.

His comment hurts worse than being devoured by a kraken. My parents frequent the other coffee place on the island. They'd rather spend money on a chain place than help out their daughter.

I need to get out of here. Why do I ever bother trying to speak with them? All they ever do is push me to do as they wish. They don't want to support *my* dreams. They want me to live out theirs.

"I need to get back to the bakery," I claim, even though the bakery is closed today.

I practically run as I push my cart out of city hall and away from them.

If I had children, I would never be mean to them the way they are with me.

Chapter 11

"Turns out the kraken isn't the only thing getting released."

Jeremy

I settle at the corner table in the bakery with my laptop. Since it's not open today, Parker said I could work here.

Anything's better than sitting in the loft trying to figure out where I went wrong with this app. I had such big hopes for *Synq*. The whole company of *Apparoo* does. And they're all looking at me – waiting for me to pull it off, like I always do. Or always have done in the past.

This time is different. Every time I open my laptop, my chest tightens. My fingers hesitate. What if I can't figure out this problem? What if this is the moment I drop the ball and everything falls apart?

I scowl when my telephone rings. I should have left it upstairs except the other board members freak out if they can't reach me. Except Eli. He knows I don't answer the phone when I'm in the zone.

Too bad I haven't been in the zone for months now.

My scowl deepens when I notice who it is. Miranda. Miranda is Eli's secretary, but she uses every excuse she can to contact me.

"What?" I bark into the phone.

"Jeremy." She giggles in that high-pitched fake way women do when they want something from you.

The sound isn't similar to the way Parker giggles. Happiness practically bursts from her when she giggles. Especially when she's giggling because I have blue frosting on my shoes. The shoes are now ruined. Worth it.

"What do you want?" I growl. I have zero patience for Miranda. She's hit on every member of the board at *Apparoo*. If Eli was in the office more often, she'd have been fired by now.

"Everyone's wondering when you'll be in the office again." Instead of giggling, this time she uses a breathy voice. It doesn't sound any more real than her laughter. I really should insist Eli fire her. It's time.

I am sick and tired of women who will do anything in their power to 'catch' a rich husband. I'm not a fish. I'm not a thing you catch and play with. I'm a human being.

"I'll be in the office when I'm in the office."

"No fair." Now she's pouting. I know her well enough to imagine her lower lip jutting out in an attempt to be sexy. It's not. "We miss you."

"Miranda," I growl. "I don't have time for this."

"I know. I know. You're a busy man. You should make time for fun."

I made time for fun this morning. Parker was panicking about finishing the gingerbread house before the deadline. And I actually had fun helping her. It was inspiring watching her creation come to life. I can honestly say I've never seen a mermaid or a pirate on a gingerbread house before but it worked.

She's amazing. And sexy. If Parker was the one on the phone trying so obviously to seduce me, I wouldn't hesitate. But the baker hates me. Ever since she found out I'm a billionaire, she's made it perfectly obvious what she thinks of me and my money.

I wonder why she has an issue with money. I wonder how her skin feels. How would she react if I pulled her into my arms and kissed her?

My cock grows and hardens. It wants to know how it feels when buried deep inside her. The feeling is mutual.

"Jeremy!" Miranda shouts and my cock immediately deflates. It has no interest in a gold digger. "Are you listening to me?"

"No."

"Don't be rude."

"I'm being honest. I told you I don't have time for you. If you don't have any real business with me, I'm hanging up."

"The technical team wants the specs."

"The specs for what?"

"They said you'd know."

"Did they ask you to contact me?" I can't imagine anyone from the technical team asking Miranda to reach out to me. She doesn't deign to speak to them.

"Well, no, but I heard them talking."

"You heard them talking?" The technical team is on a different floor from the executives. The floor has the best security money can buy. No one is stealing an idea from *Apparoo*. Not if I can help it.

"Kind of."

"I'm hanging up now." She starts to protest but I hit end call. And then I put my phone on 'do not disturb'. Miranda is not on the list of names of people who can interrupt me when I need to work.

I throw my phone on the table and get back to work.

The door to the kitchen bangs open from outside but I ignore it. It's probably Parker returning. Although the bakery is closed for the day, she said she'd be back after lunch to get an early start on the baking for tomorrow.

My stomach rumbles. I forgot all about lunch. I ignore it, too. I'm not going to finish coding this app if I stop working every time I'm distracted.

I concentrate on the lines of code as I try to find where I left off. The screen blurs in front of me. I yawn and rub my eyes. I'm tired, but I need to push through. But then my stomach rumbles again.

Crap. I'm not getting any work done until I've had a bite to eat. I think I have a protein bar in one of my bags. I'll grab it and be back to work in less than five minutes.

I push to my feet and make my way to the kitchen.

"Stupid, idiotic people," Parker mutters as she slams the door of the refrigerator shut.

She picks up her bakery tools and throws them in the sink. "They think they can tell me what to do?" She switches on the water, pours in some dishwashing liquid, and glares as the soapy water rises. "I'll tell them what they can do."

"Parker," I call.

She whirls around with a scream. "Don't make me release the kraken!"

I chuckle as I raise my hands. "Don't release the kraken. It's only me. Jeremy."

She clutches her chest. "What are you doing sneaking up on me?"

"You must not have heard me over your fight with your spatulas."

She narrows her eyes on me. "I am not fighting with my spatulas."

"Okay." I cross my arms over my chest and lean against her prep table. "What are you fighting with then? Is it the refrigerator? Or maybe your wooden spoon?"

"You're not funny."

I point to her. "But you're not throwing daggers at me with your eyes anymore."

"Oh, please. If I was throwing daggers at you with my eyes, you'd be laying on the floor bleeding out while I release the kraken to devour you."

I gulp. "Devour me?"

"I can't have your blood all over my floor. Health code violation."

"You wouldn't want to violate the health code. Murder is fine. But the health code is sacred."

"Murder is totally fine when it's justified."

I lift an eyebrow. "And you're justified in murdering me?"

"Not you. My parents."

My brow wrinkles. "Your parents?"

"Yes." She nods. "The man and woman who created me. Biologically speaking. Do you think children are delivered by storks? I hope you don't expect me to give you the birds and the bees speech. I don't have the patience today."

"I do not need the birds and the bees speech."

"Phew." She runs the back of her hand over her forehead. "One less task for the day."

"Your other task is to murder your parents?"

She scowls. "No one would blame me."

"Why would no one blame you?"

Her hands fist at her hips, and a muscle in her jaw ticks. "Because they're horrible people."

I start to console her. They can't be that bad. But I stop. I know exactly how bad parents can be. My parents are an excellent example of assholes who should have never procreated.

"What did they do?"

"What didn't they do?" She flings her hands in the air and soapy water flies everywhere.

"They try to control me. They want free pies because they shouldn't have to pay their daughter for her work. But they don't bother to frequent my bakery. They'd rather go to some stupid chain coffee shop on the boardwalk than see me every day. Oh, and I should totally quit the bakery and go work for Hudson at the resort. Me? Work for someone? Not happening."

I can't make heads or tails of what she's saying. But I know better than to interrupt a woman when she's mid rant. She'll switch her anger to me faster than I can blink.

"And if I don't want to work for Hudson, I should at least be in Paris baking at a patisserie. Because they spent way too much money on my education for me to work on this island. They should have told me they wouldn't pay for my schooling if they were going to add strings afterwards."

Her chest heaves up and down as she struggles for breath. Damn it. I can't let her hyperventilate. I'm going in. Wish me luck.

I step closer and run a hand from her shoulder down to her wrist. I capture her wrist and rub my thumb against her pulse point. She gasps and I glance at her face. Her eyes are widened and her cheeks are flushed. She's never been more beautiful than now.

"I'm going to kiss you," I murmur.

She licks her lips and I moan.

"And I'm going to let you."

Thank fuck. I meld my lips to hers. They're as soft as I suspected. There's no slick lipstick filled with fake chemicals. This is all Parker.

"Let me in," I demand against her mouth.

She doesn't hesitate and my tongue swoops into her mouth. She tastes of coffee and sugar with a hint of sea. I groan and dive deeper. My blood pulses in my veins as I attempt to memorize every inch of her mouth.

She clings to my shoulders and I wrap my arms around her waist and tug until her body slams into mine. I can feel her hard nipples poking at my chest. I want to taste those. I wrench my lips from hers before trailing kisses along her jaw. She drops her head back to give me more room.

I gather the material of her sweater and begin to—

My phone rings and I swear under my breath. "Sorry, I need to answer this."

I make certain she's steady on her feet before stepping away to answer my phone. Such bad timing. Another five minutes and I would have Parker stripped naked before me.

My cock presses against my zipper. Make that three minutes.

Chapter 12

"There's no place like home. Unless someone's eaten your tree."

PARKER

I listen to Jeremy's side of the conversation as I try to catch my breath. Great glistening krakens! What a kiss! If his phone hadn't rung, I'd be naked and enjoying some sexy times right now.

"I can fly up to New York City in my private jet if you need me," Jeremy says into his phone.

New York City? Private jet?

I scowl. How did I forget he's a billionaire?

One touch of his lips against mine and I forgot everything – his money, how a man with money tried to destroy me in the past, how men with money can't be trusted.

I scowl. I am not letting this man ruin me. No way. No how. Been there. Done that. Couldn't afford to buy the t-shirt to commemorate the occasion.

Jeremy glances over his shoulder at me and smiles. *One more minute,* he mouths to me. My legs tremble and my panties dampen at the intention in his light brown eyes.

Oh boy. I need to get out of here before I forget all sense and let this man strip me naked and touch me all over. I nearly moan as visions of him doing exactly that flitter through my mind.

Knock it off, Parker. You know better.

There's only one way to handle this. I scurry toward the door and rush outside.

The kitchen is a mess and I'll probably curse Jeremy to hell and back tomorrow morning when I end up spending way too much time cleaning my baking utensils. But I don't have a choice.

Jeremy Holland is entirely too tempting. Especially since I know how soft his lips feel, how expertly he uses his tongue, how sparks ignite when his hard length presses against my stomach.

"I need to think of something else. Anything else," I mutter to myself as I march toward my apartment.

"What did you say, dear?" Lily asks and I startle with such force I nearly fall over.

She's standing next to me on the sidewalk and I didn't notice her. Huge mistake. Lily prides herself on knowing everything going on with everyone's love lives on the island. I never should have befriended her daughter, Sophia.

I force a smile. "I was wondering what you thought of the Thanksgiving pies."

She moans. "They were delicious as always. I'm already salivating over having another pie for Christmas."

My smile is definitely strained now. Christmas is even busier than Thanksgiving. I love this season – decorating the tree, the hope of snow, caroling, mistletoe, spiked cider, and the general feel of the holiday magic – but it's also the busiest time of the year for *Pirate's Pastries.* If only I could afford to hire another baker to help me out.

"Make sure to get your order in on time." I wink.

"It's on my to-do list." Her eyes narrow. "Must run. I need to speak to Sophia about her wedding."

"How are the preparations going?" And does she want me to provide the cake?

Lily rolls her eyes. "Apparently, I'm taking over."

I bite my tongue before I laugh. She's definitely taking over. Lily doesn't hesitate to go after what she wants. Her daughter is the same. Just ask me sometime how she got her brother's best friend to fall in love with her when he was determined to resist her.

"She better not be buying a dress there," Lily mutters before racing down the sidewalk.

I contemplate messaging her daughter to warn her Lily's on the way but then I notice the back door of the hardware store open and Sophia tiptoe out. She notices me and places a finger over her lips. I chuckle. Sophia and her friends were always trouble in school. I can't believe they own a successful brewery and somehow haven't managed to burn it down during a prank gone wrong.

I wave before continuing on my way to my apartment. I shiver as the cold seeps in through my light jacket. I hope it snows. There's nothing quite like Christmas with snow.

Except last year, we actually had a storm and lost electricity. I didn't manage to bake any of my pies. My stomach drops. Please, for the love of mermaids, no snowstorm this year.

Jade waves from across the street. "Parker, how are you?"

"Hi, Jade."

She waggles her eyebrows. "How is the sexy man living in your loft?"

At the reminder of Jeremy, a vision of what we did in my kitchen pops into my mind. My cheeks start to heat. I try to fight the blush from forming but it's hopeless. I have no control over the heat I feel when I think of our kiss. At least Jade is across the street and can't see my red cheeks.

"Rumor has it he helped you with your gingerbread house. Has he helped you with anything else?"

It's official. I should have used the alleyways to walk home. Beginner mistake. I forgot how each and every person on Smuggler's Hideaway – including the local realtor – feels a need to broadcast your business to the rest of the island's inhabitants.

In my defense, I don't usually walk around the streets of the town of Smuggler's Rest during the day. I'm entirely too busy. Besides, I don't even have enough money to window shop.

I dig my phone out of my pocket. "Sorry!" I shout. "I need to take this."

I keep my phone to my ear and pretend I'm in the middle of a conversation for the rest of my walk home. I don't want to chance anyone else asking questions and me blurting out how I just kissed the billionaire and it was the best kiss of my life.

The best kiss of my life? I scowl. I refuse to believe it. Too bad I suck at lying to myself.

I arrive at my apartment building. The paint is peeling, there are parts of bicycles and cars in the front lawn, and the sidewalk is cracked. Home sweet home.

This is not the life I imagined for myself while I was in culinary school, working my ass off. I had big dreams. Dreams of an apprenticeship in a patisserie in Paris. Dreams of opening my own patisserie in New York City that specializes in French bonbons. Dreams of being far, far away from my parents.

I trudge up the broken sidewalk littered with trash to the front door. It's hanging open. Granted, there isn't much crime in Smuggler's Rest – the town is the biggest on the island but it's still a small town – but it doesn't hurt to be cautious.

I don't bother with the elevator. It's been out of order since I moved here. I make my way up the stairs to the third floor. Despite walking these stairs every day and working on my feet all day, I'm winded when I reach the top floor. What I wouldn't do for a working elevator.

"Annie!" I shout as I enter the apartment.

"Why are you shouting? I'm right here."

I sigh when I notice my roommate laying on the sofa in her pajamas while eating a sugar cookie. My brow wrinkles.

"Where did you get the cookie?"

Annie doesn't buy food. She steals mine instead. I tried labeling my food. She didn't care. I tried hiding my food in my room. She rummaged through my things to find it. Now I keep my food in the kitchen at the bakery. I'm there more than I'm at home anyway.

"From the cookie tree."

"The cookie tree?" What in the name of pirates is a cookie tree?

She motions to the Christmas tree. The Christmas tree I spent an afternoon last week painstakingly decorating with sugar cookies I spent the morning baking and decorating. The Christmas tree that is now devoid of cookies.

"Did you eat all the cookies on the Christmas tree?"

"They were just hanging there."

"Hanging there? The cookies are the decoration on the tree." Because I can't afford to buy garland and tinsel, and ornaments. Not yet.

"You didn't say they were decorations."

As if it would have mattered if I had. I should have put rat poison in those cookies.

"It's a Christmas tree. It should have been obvious."

Her nose wrinkles. "Is this one of your weird things?"

"Weird things?"

"You know. Don't eat my food in the fridge. Don't go through my things in my room. Don't wear my clothes."

At the mention of clothes, I realize Annie is wearing my pajamas.

"Why are you wearing my pajamas?"

She shrugs. "Mine were dirty."

"You could have washed them."

"Why would I wash them when I can wear yours?"

"Because they're mine and don't belong to you."

She scowls. "You are so materialistic."

I'm materialistic because I don't want her wearing my clothes or eating my food? My nostrils flare and I open my mouth to shout at her. But this isn't me. I don't shout at people. I angry-bake when I'm upset.

"Whatever," I mutter and leave her to finish her cookie.

The door to my bedroom is hanging open. I count to ten before I lay into Annie for rummaging in my room again. Obviously, she was in my room. She stole my pajamas from here.

I shut the door behind me and flop down on the bed. I sigh at how comfortable it is. I stole the bed and mattress from my parents' house. It's the only thing I own worth its weight in gold. It's a good thing it's heavy or Annie would have stolen it from me already. As it is, I suspect she sleeps in here when I'm gone.

I stare at the ceiling. It's cracked and peeling. As are the walls. I've tried painting the room but I've given up. The cracks just reappear weeks later anyway.

What I wouldn't do to sleep in the loft above the bakery. It would be the perfect little setup. Live upstairs in my cute loft and work downstairs in my beloved bakery.

I sigh. Another dream that hasn't come anywhere near to true.

Life really is what happens when you're dreaming about your future.

Chapter 13

"I left the island, but I can't leave her behind."

JEREMY

I settle into my seat on my private jet and an attendant immediately bustles to me.

"Good morning. My name is Cora and I'll be your attendant for this flight. What can I get you to drink, Mr. Holland?"

I hate being referred to as Mr. Holland. Mr. Holland is my dad and I don't want to be associated with him. But I've learned not to allow familiarity – such as letting people refer to me with my first name – as it signals to them that we're somehow friends. I don't lend my 'friends' money. And I'm tired of being asked.

"Whiskey. Neat."

"Right away. And for you, Mr. Raider?"

"Coffee. Strong as you can make it."

She hurries away and I scoff at Eli. "Coffee? I stock my jet with *Buccaneer's Whiskey* and you choose coffee?"

He grunts. "First of all, you stock your jet with my whiskey because *Buccaneer's* is the best damn whiskey money can buy."

He's not wrong. His brother, Jaxon, is the master distiller and he's a genius.

"And…" He breaks off to yawn. "Having a baby is exhausting."

"And you wouldn't have it any other way."

He grins. "Stephanie's worth the loss of sleep."

My stomach burns. Why is my stomach burning? I can't possibly be jealous. I don't want children. I'd have to find a woman first, and I know from experience women can't see past the money to the real me.

What about Parker?

Our kiss was the hottest thing I've experienced in years. Maybe ever. Her soft lips and taste of coffee and sugar with a hint of sea mesmerized me.

I was ready to strip her bare and taste and touch every single inch of her. Considering her reaction to the kiss, I bet she goes wild in the bedroom. Or on the floor of her kitchen.

But then she ran away. The second I turned my back, she was gone. She didn't say goodbye. She disappeared.

And I couldn't chase her since I have no idea where she lives. I could probably ask Eli but considering Paisley has been trying not-so-subtly to matchmake me with Parker since I arrived on the island, I didn't want to chance it.

"Why are you scowling?" Eli asks.

Cora arrives with our drinks before I can answer. I swirl the whiskey in the glass. This glass is crystal. It's beautiful and elegant. And yet I find I prefer the plastic cups with mermaids on them in Parker's apartment.

Damn it. I can't spend two minutes out of her company without thinking of her. Maybe she's one of those sea creatures she loves so much. Is there a sea creature that can bewitch men? Perhaps a mermaid.

"Jeremy," Eli grumbles. "Answer my question. Are you worried about the *Synq* app? How is the development going? You said you'd be finished by the end of Thanksgiving weekend, but Thanksgiving has come and gone and you're still on Smuggler's Hideaway working on it."

I jump at the chance to change the subject away from all my failures concerning the app. "Are you trying to get rid of me?"

"Hell, no. I love having you nearby. I've missed you this past year."

"You're the one who moved away."

"Worth it." He has the soft, infatuated look of a man in love on his face again.

My chest burns. I am not jealous. I don't want to live on Smuggler's Hideaway. I don't want a woman who loves me or a child.

I cut all of those ideas out of my dreams after my parents did what they did. Being biologically related to a person doesn't necessarily equal unconditional love. My parents' 'love' for me wasn't selfless in the least once I made my first million.

But Parker isn't the same. She isn't after my money.

And there I go fantasizing about the curvy baker again. This needs to stop. Maybe once we've spent a night exploring each other's bodies, I'll be cured of this obsession. Good plan. I smile.

"What are you smiling about?"

I wipe my smile from my face.

Eli wags a finger at me. "You can't hide from me. I've known you since our first day of college. I was there when you were curled up on the bathroom floor next to the toilet, naked and convinced you were dying."

"We agreed that incident never happened."

He barks out a laugh. "I will never agree to forget you bet the RA you could eat six packages of ramen noodles in less than five minutes."

"The resident assistant was an asshole."

"He wasn't an asshole for catching you sneaking back into the dorms at two a.m."

"It wasn't as if I was out partying. I was in the computer lab working."

"Geek."

"Geek who developed an app that made you a fortune."

"Speaking of which, you never answered my question about how the development of *Synq* is going."

Damn. Eli could always talk circles around me. There's a reason I hid out in the computer lab for most of college after all.

Cora clears her throat. "Gentlemen, we are beginning our descent into LaGuardia."

Saved by the bell. I busy myself finishing my drink, putting away the papers I got out but never touched, and righting my chair.

"It's cute you think this conversation is over," Eli says as the wheels hit the tarmac.

I pretend not to hear him. What else am I going to do? Admit I'm staring down burnout? Tell him I haven't been able to code more than a couple of lines since I arrived on Smuggler's Hideaway?

Eli is my best friend, and I trust him with my life, but some things are too private to share.

Cora opens the door to the jet and lowers the stairs. "The helicopter is waiting as requested."

I nod my thanks as I pass her. A car is waiting at the bottom of the stairs to drive us to the helicopter. Another reprieve. Eli and I have learned you don't discuss business with anyone else around. Not even a driver who's pretending to listen to a baseball game.

Five minutes later, we're in our seats in the helicopter and making our way to Manhattan.

"Are you ready for this meeting?" I ask Eli when we land, less than ten minutes later.

As the CFO, Eli is the board member who usually handles investor meetings. Unfortunately, investors inevitably request I'm in attendance as well since I'm the CEO and the person who dreams up and develops the apps that have made *Apparoo* into a multi-billion dollar enterprise.

"When am I not ready?" Eli answers as we settle into the limo waiting to drive us from the Downtown Manhattan Heliport to the Four Seasons Hotel in Tribeca.

"When you have baby spit-up on your suit jacket."

"Shit." He whips off his jacket. "Where is it? Grab me some club soda from the bar."

I burst into laughter. "Got you."

"Asshole," he mutters as he puts his jacket back on but he's smiling and not asking me how development on the app is going. Win.

We arrive at the Four Seasons in less than ten minutes.

I glance up at the building. It's a slender limestone-and-concrete tower that screams 1920s elegance. The entrance with its arched, wrought-iron accents and subtle Art Deco vine-like sconces used to awe me.

Would it awe Parker? She doesn't seem impressed by my money. But is it a lie? Is her hatred of my billionaire status a trick to gain my attention? I refuse to believe it.

We enter the double-height lobby with its patterned marble floor and walnut wood panels. The real grandeur of the space is created by the rotunda ceiling, finished in silver leaf.

Would Parker find the space grand or pretentious? Probably pretentious. She has no time for decorations that don't involve Christmas or baking.

Eli elbows me. "Investors ahead."

I button my jacket as they approach. I want to fiddle with my tie but the move would signal nervousness. I'm not nervous. I'm annoyed at having to be here.

I'd rather be back in Smuggler's Hideaway working in the corner of *Pirate's Pastries* surrounded by the scent of coffee and chocolate and cinnamon with a chance Parker would show her face. Probably with flour smudges on it.

And there I go fantasizing about the baker again. I need to get the woman out of my mind. What if the only way to stop obsessing about Parker is by sleeping with her? Then, I volunteer as tribute.

My cock twitches in my pants. I clear my throat and force thoughts of sexy, shapely bakers out of my mind. Soon. I promise my cock. Soon, we'll have her beneath us, screaming our name.

Chapter 14

"Nothing says I'm sorry like chili cookies and a runaway otter."

PARKER

I stare down at the coffee tray I prepared. Is this overkill? Do I seriously need to apologize to Jeremy?

You ran away after he kissed you until your toes curled.

My toes did not curl. Okay, fine. Maybe a little bit. I blow out a breath. And I definitely ran away.

I guess I'm apologizing. And there's no better apology than freshly brewed coffee and my Kringle Kraken Crunch – spiced cookies with a surprise swirl of chili.

I snatch the key for the loft upstairs from its spot before making my way outside to the entrance. I knock, but when no one answers, I let myself in.

Jeremy is probably working and didn't hear me. Or maybe he ignored the knock. All the movies would have me believe software engineers are in their own little world when they're coding.

"Hello," I call as I knock on the door upstairs.

I nibble on my lip as I contemplate my next steps. Technically, I'm the landlady and can enter the loft, but I'm supposed to limit my entries to 'emergencies'. Is an apology an 'emergency'? Close enough.

"Jeremy?" I call as I enter. I set the tray down on the kitchen counter. "Are you home?"

Here I am worried I've upset him, and he's not even here. I haven't heard any gossip about where he's at today. Did he leave the island without letting me know? I'm not merely some girl he kissed. I'm also the landlady. He should have told me if he was leaving early.

I search the area, but considering it's an open loft, it's not long before I realize the place is empty. Did he move out?

His laptop is nowhere to be seen, and the place feels cold and empty. My heart pounds in my chest. He left. Without saying goodbye.

Hold on, Parker. You're overreacting.

I probably am. I make my way to the closet. Several suits are hanging up and there are two pairs of leather shoes on the floor. What does he need three suits for? He wears jeans and t-shirts most of the time.

Duh, Parker. He's a billionaire.

What does being a billionaire have to do with anything? My gaze lands on the nightstand next to the bed. There are two watches on top of it. I step closer.

Sweet siren songs. I know these brands. I've seen them advertised on television. I could sell one and have enough money to pay my mortgage for a few years.

I look back at the tray of coffee and cookies I brought as an apology. Jeremy would probably laugh at this peace offering. It's cheap and pathetic compared to his billionaire lifestyle.

I snatch the tray as I retreat from the loft. There's no need to apologize. Jeremy probably hasn't given our kiss a second thought since it happened. He's a billionaire. Women throw themselves at him all the time. Including me, apparently.

I can't believe I fell for it again. I know better than to believe a word that comes out of a billionaire's mouth. Fooled again.

I return to the bakery and do the one thing guaranteed to make me smile. I steal Viking from *Smuggler's Cove,* the restaurant next door, and bring him home.

Although I claim ownership of the adorable otter, I share him with the restaurant since it's impossible for me to have him full-time in the bakery. And I can't leave him in my apartment. Annie would auction him off to the highest bidder.

Viking doesn't hesitate to jump into my arms. I cuddle him close. Animals are better than humans. Their love is truly unconditional.

I kiss Viking before placing him in his bed on the floor in the kitchen. It's time to get some Christmas baking done. I find my Christmas playlist and switch it on.

I rub my hands together. What to make first? The choices are endless.

Yule Tide Treasures – jewel-toned sugar cookies with edible glitter. *Merry Mermaid Macaroons* – coconut macaroons with blue and sea-green drizzle. *Frosted Sea Foam Swirls* – mint and vanilla meringue kisses. *Snow-drift Sirens* – white chocolate-dipped shortbread with sea salt flakes. *North Pole Narwhal Nibbles* – sugar cookies shaped like narwhals with candy cane stripes. *Coral Cane Cookies* – peppermint-flavored cookies shaped like coral. And *Gingerbeard Men* – pirate versions of gingerbread men, including an eyepatch, of course.

Oh, who am I kidding? I'm going to make them all.

Soon enough, the kitchen is filled with all my favorite baking scents. Sugar, spice, chocolate. Sigh. I love them all. Just ask my hips. They'll tell you.

Holly joins me in the kitchen. "It smells incredible in here."

"I started the Christmas baking."

Her eyes light up with excitement. "Really? Can I help?"

"As long as you continue to serve the customers in the café."

She bobs her head. "I can do it. I'll run to the café whenever the bell over the door rings."

"Okay." I consider the cookies I'm making. Sugar cookies will be the easiest for her if she has to rush away to deal with customers. "Let me show you how to shape the *Yule Tide Treasures* and decorate them."

In no time, she's covered in as much flour as I am.

"You have flour in your hair."

Her smile is blinding. "I don't care. I haven't had this much fun in forever."

I roll my eyes. She's nineteen. Her forever hasn't been very long.

She nudges me. "I'm serious. What could be better than listening to Christmas music in the background while baking cookies with the scent of sugar and chocolate surrounding us?"

"Baking is the best. If you want to learn more, I'm happy to teach you."

"Seriously?"

"Yep. If I can find someone to help out in the café, I'll teach you all I know."

"My friend, Cindy, is looking for a job."

"I thought she worked at *Mermaid Mini Golf*."

"Not enough hours in the winter."

"Okay. If she's willing to work for your wage, I'll hire her."

"Yes!" She whoops. "I'm learning how to bake."

Her excitement warms me. Most people think baking is for old women or stay-at-home wives. It's way more. Baked goods can brighten a person's day. Help you celebrate a special occasion. And comfort you when you're down.

The bell over the door rings and I nod to the café. "Get the door. We'll discuss this more later."

"Promise?"

"Promise."

While she handles the customer, I start work on my *gingerbeard men.* I have plenty of gingerbread dough left over from the gingerbread house competition, so I don't need a bunch of time to get these finished.

I'm removing the gingerbeard men from the oven when the back door opens.

"There's no fire here. It's a bit of smoke, is all."

A man chuckles, and I freeze. I know that chuckle. I whirl around.

"Jeremy? What are you doing here?"

"I live above the bakery, or have you forgotten?"

I scowl. "I haven't forgotten, but you weren't around today. I thought you might have left."

I ignore how those words burn through me. He didn't leave. There's no reason to overreact.

Because he's not mine to overreact about. We kissed once. One whole time. *Slow your roll, Parker.*

"I had an appointment in New York City today."

My eyes widen. New York City? He was here yesterday afternoon and he's back already. How?

"You were in New York today? Did you leave last night?"

He pulls at the tie around his neck until it loosens. Holy pirates stealing their bounty. How in the world did I miss that he's wearing a three-piece suit?

Jeremy in jeans and a t-shirt is sexy. Jeremy in a three-piece suit is out of this world sexy. The material clings to his body as if it was made for him. What am I thinking? It probably was.

He smiles and those matching dimples come out and I forget to breathe. If mermaids could walk on land, they'd be beating down my door to charm this man.

"Left this morning. Took the jet into LaGuardia and heli-coptered into Manhattan."

I blink. The Christmas music must be affecting my hearing. He did not say he helicoptered into Manhattan. A helicopter? I swallow. It's exactly what a billionaire would do.

Good reminder. Jeremy Holland is not the man for me. It doesn't matter how much my toes curl from his kisses. Or how my breath catches when he flashes me those dimples or how sparks ignite whenever we touch. The man is out of my league.

He steps closer and gazes down at the baking sheet. "Your gingerbread men resemble pirates."

"Wait until I add the eyepatch." He chuckles. "And they're not gingerbread men. They're gingerbeard men."

"Of…" His eyes narrow as he trails off. "I hate to say it, Parker, but I think you have a rodent problem." He digs his phone out of his pocket. "Shall I call an exterminator?"

I slap the phone out of his hand. "Don't you dare call an exterminator on Viking."

"You named your rat?"

"Why does everyone think Viking's a rat? Do they not teach biology in high school anymore?" I kneel down. "Viking, come here and meet Jeremy."

Jeremy inches backward. "Um, I don't need to meet your rat."

"I told you. Viking isn't a rat." Viking also isn't coming when he's called. I grab a gingerbeard man from the tray and break off a piece. "Viking. I have a cookie for you."

Viking loses his shyness in zero point five seconds. He scurries out from his hiding space underneath the prepping station and rushes to me.

"AGH!" Jeremy shouts as he sprints to the back door. He fiddles with the doorknob. In his panic, he seems to have forgotten how to open a door. "Don't let it kill me."

I lift Viking into my arms and cuddle him. "Did you hear the silly man? He thinks you're a killer."

I advance toward Jeremy and his eyes nearly bug out of his face as he plasters himself to the door. "You're as bad as Eli. Does money turn you into a wimp?"

He growls. "I'm not a wimp."

I raise an eyebrow. "And you're not afraid of the cutest animal in the history of animals either."

"I'm not afraid. But I need to…" The door opens and he stumbles outside.

"If this is you not afraid, I don't want to watch what happens when you are afraid," I holler after him.

I shut the door behind him and burst into laughter. I guess Jeremy is human after all. Good to know.

Maybe I need to stop punishing him for being a billionaire. He's not the billionaire who caused my heartache after all.

Maybe we can be friends.

Maybe we can kiss again.

Maybe we can be friends who kiss.

Maybe I need to stop dreaming and finish my Christmas cookies.

Chapter 15

"This detour brought to you by caffeine withdrawal and a caroling menace."

JEREMY

I rub my eyes as the lines of code begin to blur. It's getting dark outside. How long have I been at this?

It doesn't matter. I can't quit now. The investors Eli and I met with in New York City are counting on me finishing the *Synq* app and getting it to market at the start of the new year. And it's already December.

Doubt creeps in. Maybe I can't finish on time. Maybe I'm not a good enough developer to make this app a success.

No. I shake my head. I can't let doubt creep in. I can do this.

My jaw cracks with a yawn at the same time my stomach rumbles. When was the last time I ate? I pick up my coffee cup but it's empty, too.

I push to my feet and my knees creak with the motion. My entire body aches from being hunched over my computer all day as I walk to the kitchen. I frown when I notice the empty box of coffee cups.

I need caffeine. There's no way I'll be able to keep working without caffeine.

I throw on a sweatshirt, grab my keys, and hurry out the door. Shit. Cold. I forgot shoes. I rush back inside and shove my feet into a pair of sneakers.

I shiver as I walk down the stairs toward the bakery. It's not the first time I've forgotten my shoes but bare feet aren't usually a problem in California.

I notice the windows of the kitchen are dark. I try the door anyway. Locked up tight.

What now? I scan the main street of Smuggler's Rest. There. *Smuggler's Cove* is a restaurant next door. They must have coffee.

I start toward the restaurant but stop when I hear singing. I search the area and discover a group of carolers standing in the gazebo at the little park off the main street. I notice Parker in front and my feet carry me toward her before my mind can catch up.

They finish the song and move on to *Deck the Halls*. Wait a minute. This isn't *Deck the Halls*.

Deck the hulls with crates of treasure, fa-la-la-la-la, la-la-la-ARRR!

'Tis the season for pirate pleasure, fa-la-la-la-la, la-la-la-ARRR!

Don we now our sea-soaked sweaters,

Sing like drunken privateers,

Sailing home with salted letters, fa-la-la-la-la, la-la-la-CHEERS!

I chuckle. Only on Smuggler's Hideaway would they alter the lyrics of *Deck the Halls* to refer to treasure and pirates. Parker notices me and waves.

The song finishes and she steps forward. She begins to sing and I'm mesmerized.

Have yourself a sea-salty little Christmas,
Let your anchor drop…
From now on, our tides will gently rock…

She has the voice of an angel. I move closer until I can see her bright blue eyes are filled with happiness. Her long brown hair is piled onto her head, showcasing her long neck. A neck I want to nibble on until she's squirming beneath me.

The sweater dress she's wearing clings to her body and shows off all her curves. Curves I've been dreaming about since the first time we met. My cock strains against my zipper in a bid to get closer to her.

It's time to set my plan in motion to get Parker out of my system by spending a glorious night with her. Maybe two nights. Three nights would be perfectly fine with me as well.

But I don't do long term. I've learned my lesson there. Besides, I'm not in Smuggler's Hideaway to stay. Parker and I can have a glorious affair only for the season. Sounds perfect.

The music stops and Parker bounds down the stairs of the gazebo toward me.

"It's alive!"

"Why wouldn't I be alive?"

She rolls her eyes. "Because you've been barricaded in the loft since you returned from New York."

"I wasn't barricaded in the loft. But if I was, it's because I was trying to stay safe from vicious creatures."

She clutches her chest. "Vicious creatures? Viking is the sweetest of the Smuggler's Hideaway mascots."

I snort. "We're discussing Smuggler's Hideaway, the other mascots are probably krakens."

"Don't be silly. Two krakens can't live this close together."

"Pardon me. My knowledge of krakens isn't what it should be."

She bounces on her toes. "Good thing I'm here to set you straight."

"Hold on. You said mascots."

"Yep. Every town on Smuggler's Hideaway has a live mascot."

"You weren't kidding."

She frowns. "There is no joking about live mascots."

"Of course. My mistake. But, out of curiosity, what are the other mascots?"

I'll never admit it out loud, but I'm fascinated by Smuggler's Hideaway. Or maybe I am merely fascinated with this woman who lights up whenever she discusses her hometown.

"There's Rogue, the marshmallow-addicted raccoon. He's the mascot for Rogue's Landing. And the mascot for Pirate's Perch is Plank the dirty-mouthed parrot."

I snort. "I should have known there'd be a parrot."

"Plank is a rascal. No one's managed to steal him in years."

I must have misheard. "Steal him?"

"Yep. It's a Smuggler's Hideaway tradition to steal the mascot from another town during the summer."

"People try to steal Viking from you?"

She growls. "They can try. I'll beat them with my rolling pin before giving their body to the kraken."

She's adorable when she goes into mother bear mode. I bet she'd make a great mom. She wouldn't turn on her child. She'd be more likely to attack anyone who threatened her precious baby.

My gaze drops to her stomach. She'd be gorgeous with a pregnant belly. I bet she'd glow while pregnant.

My head rears back. What is wrong with me? Pregnant belly? I don't do relationships. Why the hell am I fantasizing about Parker being pregnant?

Parker grasps my forearm. "What's wrong? You look like you saw a ghost." She scans the area. "I hope it wasn't Margaret Hale. She's supposed to stick to Smuggler's Grotto." She shivers.

"Who is Margaret Hale?"

"She was the daughter of the lighthouse keeper. She was in love with the pirate Black Jack, but when her father discovered their secret affair, he arranged for her to marry someone else. On the night of her wedding, Black Jack kidnapped her, intending to escape the island by boat. But a violent storm rolled in, trapping them inside the grotto. And now Margaret's ghost wanders the grotto."

"What happens if she leaves the grotto?"

"I don't know. She's never escaped before."

"I didn't see a ghost, so I think we're safe."

"Phew. What are you doing outside anyway?"

"Searching for coffee."

Parker giggles. "I should have known. The workaholic needs his coffee." She motions toward the bakery. "Come on. I'll make you a cup."

We walk a few steps before she screeches to a halt.

"What's wrong? Did you see a ghost?" Words I never thought I'd ask before.

"No." She points to the sky. "Look."

I glance up and something cold and wet hits my eye. "Yuck."

"Don't be a fuddy duddy. It's snow." She throws out her arms and whirls around in circles. "Don't you love snow?"

"It's cold."

She stops to stare at me. "It's cold?"

I shiver and stuff my hands in my pockets. "I'm cold."

She rolls her eyes. "You're such a California boy."

I frown. "There's nothing wrong with a California boy."

"Unless you don't enjoy snow."

"You wouldn't enjoy snow either if you got stuck in New York City for New Year's Eve."

She sighs. "New York City on New Year's Eve sounds magical."

"Not when you're stuck on the jetway at LaGuardia."

"I get your point. But we are not stuck on a jetway. We're in Smuggler's Hideaway and it's nearly Christmas. Look." She points to the Christmas decorations. "Don't they look romantic with flakes of snow on them?"

I shrug. "I guess."

"I will change your mind. Tilt your head back."

"Why?"

"Why?" She grumbles before elbowing me. "To catch a snowflake on your tongue."

"It's cold and wet. Why would I want to catch a snowflake on my tongue?"

"Stop being Mr. Scrooge. I'll show you." She tilts her head back and sticks out her tongue. A snowflake falls on it and she jumps for joy. "Now, it's your turn."

"Fine," I mutter before tilting my head back and opening my mouth. A snowflake immediately falls on my tongue. "Cold. Wet."

"I give up. You are officially Mr. Scrooge."

"At least I don't have a crooked nose and wear pince-nez glasses."

She rakes her gaze over me. "You are one of the better looking Scrooges."

"You know a lot of Scrooges, do you?"

"Yes, I make a habit of befriending one every Christmas season and working with them until they realize the errors of their ways."

"In other words, I'm your little project."

Her nose wrinkles. "I wouldn't say little."

I bark out a laugh. The sound surprises me. Less than an hour ago, I was stressed and questioning all of my life's decisions. Parker has the ability to cheer me up without trying.

Instead of fighting her influence, maybe I should lean into it. After all, I deserve a nice Christmas for a change. And a Christmas season spent with Parker as my lover would be very nice indeed.

Chapter 16

"Dinner is not necessarily a date. Not even if a fancy car's involved."

PARKER

I raise my hands in the air and stretch my back. I moan as the motion causes muscles that haven't moved in hours to contract.

"Do you need a backrub?" Jeremy asks and I clutch my chest before whirling around to face him.

"You shouldn't sneak up on me."

"The door was open."

Maybe because I had a tiny mishap with my Merry Mermaid Macaroons. Macaroons are delicate. I shouldn't have used a blowtorch to caramelize the sea-green drizzle. They were perfect as they were. But I wanted to make them even better.

Perfectionists should not have access to blowtorches.

"I forgot." Liar. Liar. Macaroons on fire. "Do you need coffee? Holly's working in the café. She can make you one. No charge."

"Actually." He shoves his hands in his pockets and rolls back onto his heels. "I had a question."

"If it's whether I can remove the batteries from the smoke alarms to stop their insistent blaring, the answer is no. The fire department gets mad when I fiddle with the smoke alarms. The last time it happened, they threatened to cut off my supply of sugar. No one cuts off a baker's supply of sugar."

He chuckles. "I have no intention of touching your smoke alarms or your sugar supply."

"Good. You may live."

"Thank you, my bakery queen." He bows.

"Finally! Someone who understands my need to be referred to as queen."

"I'll call you queen from now on if you stop referring to me as Scrooge."

I scratch my chin as I pretend to contemplate his offer. "Sorry. No deal. You are a Scrooge and as such deserve to be referred to as one. Stop being a Scrooge and I'll stop calling you Scrooge."

"Not enjoying snow – which is cold and wet – doesn't make me a Scrooge."

I lift an eyebrow. "What about complaining about me singing Christmas Carols?"

"You were singing about pirates staggering."

"And? What's your point? Pirates do stagger."

"Pirates aren't Christmassy."

"They are when they've been drinking Christmas moonshine all night."

"Everyone in Smuggler's Hideaway sure loves to discuss moonshine."

I freeze. "Have you not sampled any of Smuggler's Hideaway's moonshine yet? Your buddy Eli makes several flavors at *Buccaneer's Whiskey & Distillery*."

He shivers. "I learned freshman year of college not to drink anything Eli offers me ever again."

"Landlubbers always fall for it."

"Fall for what?"

My kitchen timer goes off and I rush to my oven. This batch of macaroons is perfect. I remove the tray and set it on the table. Once they've cooled, I'll fill them with green buttercream. The red and green combination is perfect for Christmas.

"Go ahead and get your coffee." I motion to the café without lifting my gaze from my perfectly round perfections.

Jeremy clears his throat. "Actually..."

When he doesn't finish, I lift my head and meet his gaze. "Actually?"

"I wanted to invite you to dinner."

"Wanted to or still do?"

He smiles and my knees go weak when those dimples make an appearance. Somewhere I can hear an alarm shouting danger but I ignore it. I have a lot of experience in ignoring alarms.

"Still do." He motions to the table littered with cookies and trays and mixing bowls. "You could use a break. You work too hard."

I snort. "Pot meet kettle."

"I'm admitting I could use a break. What about you?"

Those light brown eyes focus on me and I can't say no. Let's face it. I'd have an easier time evading a Kraken than saying no to Jeremy Holland.

"Fine." He chuckles. "What?"

"I'm not used to women reluctantly saying yes to a dinner invitation with me."

I scowl. "I'm not most women."

I have no interest in chasing Jeremy for his money. He can keep it. Money only causes problems. Witness what assholes my parents have grown into since their little girl didn't become the famous pastry chef they expected her to after spending a 'fortune' on culinary school.

"I'll pick you up at six at your place."

Panic grips me. No way, no how is Jeremy the billionaire picking me up at my place, where he will discover how dreary and depressing my living accommodations are.

"I'll meet you here at six."

He contemplates me for a long moment before agreeing. "Okay. But I'm driving."

Joke's on him. There's no need to drive. All the restaurants in Smuggler's Rest are within walking distance of my bakery.

The rest of the day flies by. Before I know it, it's five minutes to six and I'm standing in the kitchen fiddling with my sleeves.

I shouldn't have worn this sweater dress. I was wearing it the other day when I went caroling. *And* Jeremy saw me in it.

But I didn't have any other outfit that wasn't stained or meant for the summer. It's not as if I'm used to having dinner with a handsome billionaire in the winter. Or any other time of the year, for that matter.

The door opens and Jeremy strides in wearing one of those fancy suits I saw hanging in his apartment. Crap on a pirate's moonshine. I am seriously underdressed. Maybe we should call this whole thing off.

"Is this a date?" I blurt out instead. *Way to go, Parker.* Super smooth operator.

He grins as he leans over to kiss my cheek. "It's whatever you want it to be."

"Whatever I want it to be?" I tap my chin. "The possibilities are endless."

"But you should know I don't do long-term relationships."

I study his face. His brown eyes are cold, and his jaw is set. There's a story there but I don't think I'll be hearing it.

"Gotcha. Scrooge doesn't do relationships."

It's not as if Mr. Billionaire Tech Developer is going to fall in love with little old me and give up his glamorous life in California for Smuggler's Hideaway anyway.

"I will get you to stop calling me Scrooge," he grumbles.

"You can try," I sing as I make my way out of the kitchen to the street. My brow wrinkles when I notice the fancy car waiting at the curb. "We don't need to drive. Everything in Smuggler's Rest is within walking distance."

He opens the car door and ushers me inside. "We're not staying in Smuggler's Rest."

"Where are we going?" I ask once he's situated behind the driver's seat.

"*Hideaway Haven Resort.*"

"Hudson's resort?"

"You know Hudson Clark?"

"Don't get excited, Scrooge. Hudson and I grew up on the island together. All islanders know each other."

He growls. "You didn't date, did you?"

"Ha! Me date Hudson, the high school quarterback? Not in a million years. Besides, he's been in love with Nova forever."

"They just had a baby, right?"

"Yep. Iliana. Do you know Hudson?"

I'm convinced there's a secret club that all billionaires and famous sportspeople and movie stars and pop idols belong to. I bet all of them were the cool kids in high school, too. Not me.

I was usually sneaking into the school kitchens to study how they cooked. The principal was not amused when I missed my AP English exam because I was in the middle of stuffing a turkey and couldn't stop without ruining the meal.

"I met him at Thanksgiving at Eli's house."

"I should have known. Paisley and Nova are two of the terrible five."

"The terrible five?"

"Sophia, Chloe, Maya, Nova, and Paisley. The five women own *Five Fathoms Brewing* now. But I remember when they were running around the island causing havoc and mayhem."

"They're still causing havoc and mayhem. They made us play musical chairs during dinner. Whoever lost had to wear a turkey hat and tell an amusing family secret. If no one laughed, they lost the next round as well."

"Sounds better than my Thanksgiving dinner."

"What did you do for the holiday?"

I had to open my big fat mouth? Too bad I don't have a cookie to stuff in it.

"Nothing much."

"Nothing much?" Unfortunately, we've arrived at the resort and he parks before switching his full attention to me. "What is nothing much?"

Color me shipwrecked. Me and my big mouth will now be retiring for the evening. No more speaking whatsoever.

Jeremy reaches across the console to pinch my chin. "Parker," he grumbles. "Answer my question."

"Fine. I worked all morning and then went home and slept all afternoon. Happy now?"

He scowls. "No, I'm not happy. I should have invited you to spend Thanksgiving with me and Eli's family."

I roll my eyes. "We barely knew each other then."

"And you hated me."

I sigh. "I don't hate you."

Hate what his money stands for? Maybe. But Jeremy the person? I could never hate him. No matter how much money he has. And no matter how I've tried. And, boy, have I tried.

"Good because I don't enjoy kissing women who hate me."

His gaze drops to my lips and my breath catches. Do I want him to kiss me? He made it perfectly clear this relationship can't be anything but temporary.

I don't usually indulge in one-night stands. But what can it hurt? It's not as if I'm going to fall in love with a billionaire. I'm not an idiot.

I palm his neck and draw him near until our lips meet. He growls and takes over. My entire body tingles as his tongue slips into my mouth.

It's official. I'm trying this one-night stand thing.

Chapter 17

"Turns out, I like my sugar with a side of sass and thigh-highs."

JEREMY

I tilt Parker's head until I have the angle I want. The angle allows me to dive deep into her mouth. Her sweet, sumptuous mouth, I can't get enough of. I need to memorize every inch of it.

This will probably be the last chance I have to taste her coffee and sugar flavor. I'm not in town for long. And I don't do repeats. Repeats lead to women having 'ideas about relationships'. And I was serious. I don't do relationships.

I pull her closer but she grunts. I wrench my lips from hers. Hers are swollen and red from my kisses. She's never looked more beautiful.

"What?" I bark out since I'm barely capable of speaking. Not with my cock pounding in my pants.

"The console's in the way."

"Shit. We can't have sex in a parking lot."

"Really?" She waggles her eyebrows. "Sex in a car is a rite of passage in Smuggler's Hideaway."

"I'm not a fucking teenager hiding his sex life from his parents."

She giggles. "Do your parents comment on your sex life often?"

I shrug. "If they do, I wouldn't know. I'm not in contact with them."

She opens her mouth as if to ask why but snaps it shut nearly as quickly. Good. Since I won't answer any of her questions anyway. My parents and the shit storm they caused is not a topic I discuss with anyone.

Not even sweet little bakers I want to devour.

She offers me her hand instead. "Welcome to the shitty parents' club. I don't have a membership card on me. I'll have to mail it to you."

I chuckle. I can't believe I'm laughing when the subject is my parents but if there's anyone who can make me laugh when I'm usually annoyed, it's Parker.

I shake her hand. It's not soft like the models I'm used to. She has callouses and scars from burns. She's a real woman. Someone who's determined to pave her own destiny in life. It's nearly as sexy as her chest in the sweater dress she's wearing.

"Are you hungry?"

She glances up at me from beneath her lashes. "Depends on what's on the menu."

I debate my answer. I usually wine and dine women before I take them to bed. But there's nothing usual about Parker.

"You."

Her eyes widen. "I'm on the menu?"

I nip her chin before I growl into her ear, "I plan to taste every inch of your body tonight." She shivers in response. Good. I love a responsive woman.

"I-I-I wouldn't say no," she stutters.

"The question is. Do you want dinner first?"

She doesn't hesitate to answer, "I have a tray full of cookies not pretty enough to sell. We can snack on those if we get hungry."

Good enough for me. I switch on the car and whip out of the parking spot.

She giggles as she reaches for the handle to steady herself. "There's no hurry."

Every inch of me aches for her. "Disagree."

"At least slow down so you don't run over Sammy."

"Who the hell is Sammy? Another ghost?"

"Don't be silly. Sammy isn't a ghost. Sammy's a seal."

I cough to hide my amusement. I don't want Parker to think I'm making fun of Smuggler's Hideaway again. "A seal?"

"Yep. Sammy doesn't think much of being on his own in the ocean. He prefers to laze around the island and get fed by the locals and tourists."

"Where's his home?"

"He doesn't have one. He enjoys sleeping in the middle of the road and on people's porches."

"And I thought Viking was bad."

"No making fun of my otter."

She slaps my chest. I capture her hand and thread my fingers through hers. Holding hands usually feels juvenile to me, but I can't stop myself from touching Parker. Not even when I'm driving and should be paying attention to potential seal sightings.

We fall into silence. I don't know why Parker is quiet but personally, I'm finding it hard to think and drive while all of the blood in my brain has moved south to my cock.

We arrive in Smuggler's Rest in less than ten minutes. I park behind the bakery. I was supposed to return the rental car this evening but I don't give a shit about late fees or whatever penalties they throw at me. I have more important matters to handle. Such as making Parker scream.

She reaches for her door handle but I stop her. "Wait for me."

She holds up her hands. "Alrighty then."

I don't know why I told her to wait for me. I don't usually open women's doors for them. The act creates expectations and I'm all about making certain no woman has any expectations when it comes to me.

I open her door and she smiles up at me as she takes my hand while I help her out of the vehicle. I draw her near until her body slams into mine. She fits perfectly against me. I never would have thought a woman who's half a foot shorter than me would fit me perfectly but she does.

She shivers and I realize we're standing outside in the cold. "Come on. Let's warm you up."

I shackle her wrist and lead her to the loft. She rushes to keep up with me but I don't slow down. I can't. My cock is in charge now.

Once we're upstairs, I slam the door shut before pressing her to it.

"Two choices."

She lifts a brow. "Which are?"

"I can fuck you against the door with your dress pulled up around your waist. Or I can fuck you in the bed."

"Why can't we do both?"

I moan. This is my kind of woman. Someone who enjoys sex and isn't ashamed of it.

I slam my hands on the wall next to the door to cage her in. "Tell me you aren't wearing stockings."

"I'm not wearing stockings."

I rake my gaze down her body until I reach her legs, which are clearly covered in stockings.

She nibbles on her bottom lip. "They're thigh-highs."

I moan. "I'm fucking you with your heels and those thigh-highs on."

Her breath hitches. "Yes, please."

I'm hard as steel. There's nothing sexier than a woman begging during sex. "I love it when you beg."

"I wasn't begging."

"But you will be."

She sniffs and lifts her perky little nose in the air. "I will not."

I smirk. "This is going to be fun."

"Promises. Pro—"

I slam my mouth to hers before she can finish her taunt. She gasps and I thrust my tongue inside. Her taste has me moaning. Coffee, sugar, and a hint of sea. It's as unique as Parker is.

She grasps my shoulders and I yank my lips from hers. "Hands on the wall."

"But I want to touch you," she pouts.

"And you will." She grins. "When I allow it."

"Scrooge is bossy."

"I'm in control here. Do you have a problem with me being in charge?"

She contemplates me for a long moment and my stomach drops. Fuck. She's going to say no. She's going to stop this before we can get started.

The water in the shower isn't cold enough to handle how hard it will be for me to walk away from her. But I will. I don't push women against their will.

"Will you give me an orgasm?"

"I'll give you as many as you want."

"As many as I want? Don't oversell it, Scrooge."

I growl. "Stop calling me Scrooge."

"Start giving me orgasms."

"You'll listen to my orders? You accept I'm in control?"

"As long as you don't deny me an orgasm, we're good."

Relief pours through me. She's not saying no. In fact, she's wriggling against me, trying to get some relief.

"Be still."

Her breath hitches and she stills. Huh. Someone gets off on being ordered around. This night is getting better and better.

"Reach down and pull your dress up until it's bunched around your waist."

She stares into my eyes as she does exactly as I say. Her blue eyes sparkle with challenge. I can't wait until they sparkle with passion.

I tear my gaze away from hers to look down. Her green dress is bunched around her waist, allowing me a clear view of her black, lace panties.

I want to rip her panties away, but ripped panties create more expectations than opening doors. I trace the skin along the edge of her thigh-highs instead and she shivers in response.

"Hands on the wall," I growl as I kneel down.

I wait until her palms are plastered against the wall before I reach for her panties. I want to taste her. I bet she's as sweet as the sugar she uses in her baking. But my cock has nearly lost its patience. Later. I'll taste every inch of her later.

I draw her panties down her legs until they fall to the ground. "Kick them away."

My cock weeps when she follows my order. "Good girl."

I enjoy the feel of the silk of her thigh-highs as I trail my hands up her legs until I reach her core. "Are you wet for me?" I ask as I dip my finger into her pussy. I moan at the moisture gathered there.

"It's been a while."

"Your dry spell is officially over, Princess."

I plunge two fingers inside her and she moans as she tries to ride them.

"Stay still," I order.

"You promised not to deny me orgasms."

"I promise you're going to come so hard you scream."

She meets my gaze. "Yes, please."

"I fucking love it when you beg." I reward her by pumping my fingers in and out of her. She bites her bottom lip and her legs tremble as she fights to stay still. "Good girl. Are you ready for your reward?"

"Yes," she breathes out. "A million gallons of moonshine, yes."

I withdraw my fingers – I'll be getting her off with them later – and reach for my belt. I open my pants and pull out my cock. I quickly don a condom before grasping her hips.

"Wrap your legs around me."

She does as I ask and now we're lined up perfectly. I notch my cock at her entrance.

"This is going to be hard and fast. We'll do slow later."

I don't give her a chance to respond before I thrust inside her all the way until my balls slap against her ass. Fuck. Fuck. Fuck. She feels better than anything I've ever felt before. She's hot and wet and her walls are tight around me.

I want to stay buried in her forever. My back tingles and my balls heat. I clench my jaw before I give in to the desire to come. Parker comes first.

"Hard and fast," I grit out before slowly withdrawing. When only the tip remains inside her wet heat, I plunge back inside.

Her breasts press against my chest as I pump into her pussy over and over again. Her head falls back and thumps against the wall. Her eyes fall closed as she takes everything I give her.

A blush travels from her cheeks down her neck to the top of her dress. I want to see where her blush ends. I want to strip her bare and touch every inch of her skin. Next time, I promise myself. Next time.

Her walls spasm around my cock. "Are you ready to come, Princess?"

"So ready."

"Open your eyes."

Her eyes flutter open and I reward her with a finger on her clit. I play with the hard nub while I continue to pound into her. Her eyes flare, and her breath gets caught in her throat.

"Come for me, Princess. Come all over my cock."

"Yes!" she shouts as her pussy strangles my cock.

Her climax triggers mine and I lose my rhythm as I explode into the condom. It's a good thing I bought a box of them today because I am not letting Parker go until I've wrung as many orgasms out of her as I can.

One time is not enough with Parker. I'm afraid forever with her won't be enough.

Chapter 18

"I woke up to cookie crumbs and questionable decisions."

PARKER

My eyes fly open as I jolt awake. I don't need an alarm clock. My body knows when it's time to get out of bed and get to work.

But this isn't my bed. And the wall of heat behind me isn't part of my usual morning routine. A wall that's currently curled up around me, making me feel safe and warm.

Slow your mermaid-loving mind, Parker.

Jeremy made things perfectly clear last night. One night only and he was done. My stomach hardens. I don't want to be done.

I've never been with a man who made me feel the things I felt last night. My body is deliciously sore and yet it aches for more.

But there's more to Jeremy than his skills in the bedroom. He's kind. He asked me to dinner last night because he thinks I work too hard. My own parents don't care how much I work.

And he's helpful. He helped me finish the gingerbread house on time, even though he obviously had no clue what he was doing.

And he doesn't take himself too seriously. Despite being a billionaire. He shrugged it off when the blue frosting – guaranteed to stain – landed on his sneaker. A sneaker I've since googled and discovered costs more than a dozen Thanksgiving pies.

"What are you thinking about so hard?" Jeremy asks in a scratchy morning voice I shouldn't think is sexy but I do. He drags his beard slowly against the sensitive skin beneath my ear. The scratch sends sparks straight to my toes.

"I… ah…" Completely forgot all the thoughts flying around in my mind when he touched me.

This is not good. I'm going to fall for this completely un-available and most certainly inappropriate man if I don't watch myself.

"I can give you a few things to think about." He rubs his hard length between my ass cheeks and those sparks turn into anticipation.

Anticipation? No. Jeremy made himself perfectly clear last night. This was a one-night stand. And one-night stands in my extremely limited experience do not include morning sex. They also don't include staying over but what do I know?

I'm tempted to give in. To roll over and let Jeremy have his wicked way with me. I never thought I'd enjoy a man who is controlling in the bedroom. I was wrong. Epically wrong.

But I don't want to blur the lines.

"I should go. I need to start baking for the day."

He squeezes my hip. "You can be thirty minutes late." He thrusts his hardness against me. "I'll make it worth your while."

"I thought you'd kick me out of bed last night. Not invite me to have morning sex."

He sighs before using his hold on my hip to roll me over. "I'm not a monster."

I force myself to meet his gaze. "No. But you were very clear. One night only."

He tugs me closer. "I've been thinking."

"Uh oh, Scrooge is thinking. Watch out, Christmas ghosts."

He rolls his eyes. "There is no such thing as a Christmas ghost."

"You're going to be scared shitless when the Ghost of Christmas Past shows up."

He tweaks my nose. "Stop teasing me. I'm trying to be serious here."

I motion for him to get on with it.

"What if our arrangement lasted longer than one night?"

My brow wrinkles. "More than one night?"

He brushes the hair from my forehead and frowns before pulling out a cookie crumb. "There are crumbs everywhere in my bed."

"Don't blame me. I'm not the one who decided to use my body as a buffet table."

His eyes heat, and his gaze drops to my naked chest. "Worth it."

My breath hitches at his expression. He's the big, bad pirate, and I'm the little mermaid who's lost her pod. I clear my throat. "I'm not cleaning your sheets."

"Still worth it."

I bite my bottom lip and gaze up at him from beneath my eyelashes. "Yeah, it was."

I can't deny it. The desire in his eyes while he feasted off my body made me feel like the most desirable woman in the world. When you're a small-town baker with more hips and ass than should be allowed, it's a heady feeling.

"Now. About our arrangement."

"We don't have an arrangement."

"Why don't we continue this affair until I leave for California?"

I open my mouth to shout yes but common sense stops me before I do. Last night changed things for me. I no longer believe Jeremy is an asshole billionaire. In fact, he's a man I could fall for. Without trying.

"This isn't a good idea."

"Why not? I'll give you as many orgasms as you want."

I rub my legs together as excitement builds in my core. Knock it off, I tell my hormones but they don't listen.

"It's a bad idea."

"Why?"

I can hardly tell him the truth. I'm afraid I'll fall in love with him if we continue to have sex.

I shake my head. I'm not going to fall in love with Jeremy. He's a billionaire. Who's shown me he's kind and helpful and doesn't take himself too seriously. Sea saints help me. I'm already falling for the man.

He palms my neck. "Come on, Parker, I'll make it worth your while."

And he'll probably break my heart. I'm still recovering from the last billionaire who broke my heart. There should be a support group to help women who are addicted to falling in love with billionaires. I can't be the only one.

"Only for the season?" The words tumble out of my mouth before I can stop them.

"Only for the season," he agrees. "Once New Year's day hits, I'll be gone from Smuggler's Hideaway and you won't be bothered with me again."

Which is exactly what I'm afraid of.

"We need some ground rules."

He adopts a serious face. "Negotiations? I'm ready."

I'm an idiot if I think I can negotiate with a man who runs a multi-billion dollar company but I don't back down. Never retreat.

"No other women while we're together."

He scowls. "I'm not a cheater."

"I didn't say you were but this isn't serious." To him at least. "Exclusivity isn't a given."

"I agree to exclusivity. What is your next demand?"

I search my mind for ideas but I don't have any. I can hardly order him not to break my heart. Not when I don't want him to know how much I care for him already. How I'm falling for him and it wouldn't take much to push me over the love cliff.

"No more making fun of Viking."

"Okay."

"And you will cuddle him."

He shivers. "Cuddle the crazy animal?"

I slap his chest and he captures my hand to place it against his heart. I can feel it beating – strong and steady. While mine is going crazy with fear and anxiety about this deal. Obviously, my feelings aren't reciprocated.

Good reminder. I will do my best to stop falling in love with him while spending time with him. How hard can it be?

"Yes, Viking is a sweetheart and you'll learn to love him."

The way I wish he would learn to love me.

I nearly groan. This sappy stuff isn't like me. I've learned my lessons about men. Except I obviously haven't.

He frowns. "I agree to try to cuddle him and maybe even like him eventually, but I draw the line at loving a furry creature with beady eyes."

"Fine."

"Fine?"

I nod.

"We have a deal?"

Against my better judgment, I agree. "We have a deal."

His eyes sparkle. "It isn't a deal until it's sealed with a kiss."

I roll my eyes. "There's always a catch."

He smiles before his head dips and his lips are on mine. He tastes of dark chocolate, espresso, and sin. All the things I love. I could get addicted to his taste. To how he growls and dives deeper as if he can't get enough of me. To how his tongue duels with mine.

His hand tightens on my neck. I learned last night this means he's done with me playing. It's time for him to be in control.

And I don't fight him. I have enough aspects of my life where I'm in control. Where I have to be the boss. Where I'm the responsible one.

If Jeremy wants to accept responsibility for providing me with pleasure, I'll let him.

Until he walks away and breaks my heart.

Chapter 19

"Focus returns. That's all this is. Probably."

JEREMY

I whistle as I dry my hair after my shower. My body is completely sated. My limbs feel loose and lumber. I'm well rested. I don't have a headache for the first time in weeks. And I'm starving. It's been a long time since I've felt this way.

It's probably why I pushed Parker to agree to continue our affair until I leave for California. Parker understands my boundaries. She won't try to trick me or trap me. She's too genuine to play those games.

My stomach rumbles, reminding me of my hunger and I snatch the plate of cookies Parker ran to the kitchen for last night. I settle in front of my computer and get to work.

A hum of excitement buzzes underneath my skin. Welcome, inspiration, my old friend. I've missed you.

Lines of code fly from my fingers. The cookies and coffee are forgotten as the *Synq* app begins to form. No longer is the app a product of my imagination. This productivity and communication app is coming into shape.

My phone buzzes on the table and Abba's *Money, Money, Money* begins to play. I hit ignore. Eli can wait.

I barely have a chance to return to my work when the phone rings again. This time, *The Imperial March* plays to indicate it's Eli calling again.

Crap. It must be important.

"What?" I bark at the phone.

Eli laughs. "You forgot."

"Forgot what?"

"We have a board meeting. You were supposed to meet me at my house thirty minutes ago."

I check my diary and swear when I realize he's right. "Sorry, I missed it."

He chuckles. "You didn't miss it. I gave you the wrong time on purpose. I knew you'd be busy developing the app."

He doesn't realize how wrong he is. Until this morning, I could barely remember what coding was, let alone how to do it. But inspiration hit me hard when Parker shimmered her sexy ass out of here this morning.

Parker. I wonder if I can sneak a few kisses from her. She's downstairs baking now. I can smell chocolate and sugar, and coffee.

My stomach rumbles again. I notice the plate of cookies is untouched. I forgot all about eating when I started working.

All the tension in my body releases. I haven't lost it. I can still develop software the same way I did in our dorm room a decade ago.

"Okay," I say to Eli. "What time is the actual board meeting?"

"In an hour. Don't make me come into town and drag you out of your place."

"I'm on my way." I end the call and slam my computer shut. An hour gives me plenty of time to visit Parker.

"Hey, you," Parker greets when I enter the kitchen. She draws a hand over her forehead, leaving a trail of flour in her wake.

I chuckle. "Hey, yourself."

I brush the flour off her forehead before pressing a quick kiss to her lips.

"Sorry. I can't touch you." She wiggles her hands. They're covered in dough and flour.

I step closer until she's crowded against the prep table. "I prefer it when you can't touch me."

Her eyes narrow. "And I prefer it when I can touch you."

I tweak her nose. "Don't lie. You love it when I'm in charge."

"Do not." Her voice is all breathy, and she's shivering.

"Shall I prove what a liar you are?"

"Not here!" she squeaks.

I scowl. "Afraid people will see us together?"

She snorts. "More like afraid our naked asses will end up in the dough and I'll have to start over."

"Dough? Kinky."

"It's not…"

I press my lips to hers before she can continue with her denial. She sighs and I swoop my tongue into her mouth. I growl when her flavor hits me. I will never experience coffee and sugar again without thinking of Parker. Of how she melts for me. Of how good it feels to bury myself deep inside her.

My cock twitches. It's on board with this plan. Who cares about the dough?

"Ahem." I ignore whoever it is. "AHEM!"

Parker shoves me away and I stumble before righting myself on the oven.

"What is it, Holly?" Parker asks.

"Someone wants to order a Christmas cake. Can you fit them in?"

"I'll be out there in a second. I just need to wash my hands."

"Wash your hands," Holly mutters. "Sure, you do."

When she's gone, Parker groans. My stomach dips. Is she embarrassed of being with me? Does she want to keep me a secret? I'm no one's dirty little secret.

"Holly is going to spread the word of how she saw us kissing to the entire island."

"Why do you care?"

"I don't care if people know we've done dirty things together, but I hate being the center of gossip."

I step closer to her. "You sure you're not embarrassed of me?"

"Are you joking? You're the one who should be embarrassed of me."

"Why would I be embarrassed of you?"

"Duh." She motions to me. "You're a sexy billionaire."

I smirk. "You think I'm sexy."

She rolls her eyes. "And I'm a chubby baker."

"You're not chubby. You're curvy. And those curves make my cock hard."

Her breath hitches. "They do?"

"To be continued. I have a meeting. I'll be back later." I waggle my eyebrows to make it clear what I plan to do 'later'.

"Later."

I kiss her cheek before strolling out of the kitchen. I dig out my phone to order a taxi before I realize I left the rental car here last night. Maybe I should keep the rental car for the rest of the time I'm on the island. It could come in handy for dates with Parker.

I drive to Eli's house. It's a good thing I know the way because the GPS tries to send me down a dirt path. Again. I'm tempted to remove the device and fiddle with the programming, but Eli is already standing on his porch waiting for me.

He smiles as I approach. "Someone has their groove back."

Paisley rushes to us. "I knew it! I knew Parker was perfect for you."

I glare at her. "Parker and I aren't together."

She snorts. "And you weren't seen canoodling this morning."

I groan. Now I understand why Parker was annoyed when Holly saw us. Holly obviously rushed to tell everyone on the island the gossip.

"I don't canoodle."

Eli crosses his arms over his chest. "You also don't get involved with women when it can get complicated and nothing spells complicated more than having sex with the woman who works downstairs from the loft you're renting. And who owns the loft."

"Who said anything about sex?"

Paisley points at my face. "The blush on your face when Eli said sex." She pumps her fist. "Yes! This is awesome. I'm the best matchmaker on the island. My friends can shove it."

"Paisley," I grumble. I wait until she meets my gaze before continuing, "I'm not on the island to stay. You shouldn't be playing with people's lives this way."

"We'll see," she sings as she skips away.

"Paisley!" I holler and start after her.

Eli blocks me. "Watch it."

"Your wife is trying to matchmake me."

"Not his wife yet," Paisley calls from somewhere in the mansion.

"I don't do relationships. You know why."

Eli frowns. "I don't agree with your reasons. Not every woman is a money-grubbing manipulator out to catch a billionaire."

"Easy for you to say. Paisley loved you before you earned your first million."

"Getting Paisley to stop hating me for a mistake I made in high school was anything but easy."

"At least you knew she didn't want you for your money."

"You should speak to Parker. Ask her what she thinks of your money."

I roll my eyes. "What she thinks of my money? I know what people think of my money. They want it."

He shakes his head. "Parker's different. Ask her."

"What do you know about it?" I grumble.

He holds up his hand. "There's no reason to go caveman on me. Parker and I have never been romantically involved. But we did go to high school together and have been friends for years."

"And?"

He shrugs. "And there are things you don't know about her that might change your perspective."

I shake my head. "Nothing will change my perspective."

"You want to die alone?"

"Everyone dies alone."

He sighs. "I don't have time to deal with this. We have a board meeting."

"What's this board meeting about anyway?" I ask as I follow him through his house to his office.

"Developments with the *Sync* app. Which we no longer have to worry about, do we?" He raises his eyebrow.

"Nope. We're good."

Because a certain woman inspired me and now the development is racing forward. My heart pounds in my chest. A woman I barely know shouldn't be able to inspire me. Especially when our relationship is temporary.

What if it doesn't stay temporary?

I shake my head. Of course, it will stay temporary. I don't have anything else to offer. I've been burned before. I don't need another lesson in heartbreak.

Chapter 20

"Welcome to Mariner's Market. Would you like some shame with that?"

P*ARKER*

I open the back door and nearly run into Jeremy. "I'm on my way out."

He plants a kiss on my cheek and my body lights up from the tiny bit of contact. This man is dangerous to my health. Worse than bingeing on an entire chocolate cake. Which I only do when the cake is lopsided. Mostly.

He grasps my hand. "Okay. Let's go."

"I'm going to the grocery store."

"I'll go with."

He can't be serious. "You're going grocery shopping?"

He shrugs. "I can do groceries."

"Oh, yeah? When was the last time you were in a grocery store?"

"Must we focus on details?"

I giggle. "I take your answer to be a million years ago."

He scowls. "How old do you think I am?"

I study his face. "Fifty?"

He dives at me to tickle my ribs. I try to bat his hands away. "Stop."

"Admit you lied."

"What did I lie about?"

He wraps an arm around my waist and draws me near. "You don't think I'm fifty."

"I don't?"

"A fifty-year-old doesn't have my stamina."

"Really?"

"Want me to prove it to you?"

I do. I most definitely do. But there's no time for sexy games. The grocery store closes soon.

"Fine." I grunt. "You're not fifty."

He kisses my forehead before releasing me. "Now, grocery shopping. Do we walk? Do we drive?"

"We can walk. *Mariner's Market* doesn't mind if I borrow a shopping cart to bring my groceries back to the bakery."

He switches directions. "We're not pushing a shopping cart across town like a bunch of beach bums."

I screech to a halt. "Are you saying I'm a beach bum? Because pushing a shopping cart across town is my jam."

He sighs. "Allow me to rephrase. Why do all the work of pushing a cart when we have a rental car at our disposal?"

He does have a point. Wheeling a cart with one rogue back wheel across the street while tourists honk at me while ignoring the speed limit is not my idea of fun. "Fine."

We drive the few blocks to *Mariner's Market*. The parking lot is nearly empty since it's December and most of the tourists have left the island. They'll be back for Christmas and New Year's but the weeks between Thanksgiving and Christmas are a welcome reprieve.

I grab a cart but Jeremy pushes me out of the way and snatches it from me. "I got it."

I dig out my phone and pull up my grocery list. Jeremy glances over my shoulder at the list and groans.

"Don't say I didn't warn you," I sing.

"Where do we start?"

"The best aisle. The bakery aisle."

We make our way through the grocery store, filling the cart with items from my list. I promise all the chocolate is for baking. None of it is for me.

It's handy having Jeremy with me. He can reach the items on the highest shelf. I usually have to climb the shelves. But I've been banned by *Mariner's Market* from climbing ever since the 'peanut butter' incident. How was I to know the jars of peanut butter were glass?

Having Jeremy around is not only handy. It feels nice. I'm usually on my own. Having a man to help out and joke with me while doing groceries feels good. Better than good.

Stop it, heart. We're not falling in love with this man.

Except you're already halfway there.

I ignore the taunt. No matter what happens my 'relationship', or whatever you want to call it, with Jeremy, has an expiration date.

"Why are there two hundred types of cereal?" Jeremy asks when he cut through the breakfast aisle.

"You really haven't been in a grocery store forever."

He picks up a box. "Elf on the Shelf: Hot Cocoa Cereal," he reads the label. "Is this breakfast or a holiday-themed dare?"

I snatch the box from him and put it back on the shelf.

He picks up another box. "Kit Kat Cereal. Do people not just eat the actual candy?"

Again, I snatch the box from him and put it back on the shelf. "It's for children."

He rears back. "Children? Parents let their kids eat candy for breakfast?"

"I…" I trail off when my gaze catches on the two people walking down the aisle toward us. Speaking of parents.

I search for an exit but we're halfway down the aisle. If we whirl around, they'll most certainly notice us. Maybe I can crawl into the grocery cart and they won't see me.

"Parker," Mom says – the disapproval clear in her voice.

Awesome. There's no escape. And Mom is in a snarky mood.

"Mom." I nod and try to keep going. I don't make it far before Dad places a hand on the cart to stop us.

"Shopping for supplies for your little bakery?" Dad practically sneers his question.

I don't go for the bait. "Yep." I try to continue but Dad's grip on the cart tightens.

"How did you graduate from culinary school without an apprenticeship?" Mom crosses her arms over her chest.

Wonderful. She's settling in for an argument about my failings in front of Jeremy, the self-made billionaire. These discussions are usually embarrassing enough. Today is going to take the cake. And not the good cake. One of those dry as bone cakes without any yummy frosting.

"The school promised us all graduates would receive apprenticeships," Dad adds.

I had an apprenticeship. In Paris. No less. At a cute little patisserie I've only seen online because guess who's never visited Paris?

I shrug. "Maybe you should ask them."

"I'm asking you."

"I have no answer for you."

Because I am not explaining to my parents what a complete idiot I was, who got used in the worst possible way. Mom and Dad wouldn't hesitate to litigate against the asshole. And then the whole world would know what a fool I am. No thanks.

"I have had enough of you, young lady." Uh oh. Mom's bringing out the young ladies.

"I'd love to stay and chat but I need to get back to work."

"Work?" Dad snorts. "You call your little bakery work?"

"Okay. Enough," Jeremy grumbles and I jump. I forgot he was standing behind me. Witnessing this entire episode. My cheeks darken as embarrassment flows through me.

Dad glares at him. "Who are you?"

Jeremy reaches for my hand and pulls me close. "I'm Parker's boyfriend and I don't appreciate your tone when you speak to her."

Mom sticks her nose in the air. "Parker is our daughter and we'll speak to her however we want."

"Wrong." Jeremy squeezes my hand. "If you can't treat *your* daughter with respect, this conversation is over."

"Who do you think you are?" Dad asks.

"I told you. I'm Parker's boyfriend. I won't allow you to disrespect her in front of me."

"Allow us?" Dad snorts. "We'll do whatever we want."

Which apparently includes embarrassing their only child in the grocery store. Instead of supporting her and, I don't know, maybe inviting her to holiday meals once in a while.

"We're leaving," Jeremy announces.

Dad's nostrils flare and his cheeks darken with anger. "You'll leave when I tell you, you can leave."

Jeremy chuckles but he is not amused. Quite the opposite. "Go ahead and try to stop me. I have a whole team of lawyers who would love to sue you for wrongful imprisonment."

Mom's brow wrinkles. "Team of lawyers? Are you a lawyer?"

Interest sparks in her eyes and I groan. When my parents aren't blaming me for wasting their money, they're pushing me to 'find a good man to keep me' – since my career is a disaster in their opinion.

Spoiler alert. I am not an object to be kept.

"Nope," Jeremy answers but he doesn't offer any further information. I nearly giggle. Mom hates it when a person withholds information. Another reason I haven't explained what happened at culinary school to her. Her irritation brings me a spark of joy.

"Who are you?"

"Parker's boyfriend."

"What's your name?"

"Jeremy."

I expect her to ask for his last name, which he won't give her, but instead she asks, "What do you do for a living?"

He shrugs. "A little bit of this. A little bit of that."

A muscle ticks in Mom's jaw. She is not getting the information she wants. I nearly clap to encourage 'my boyfriend'.

The intercom crackles before an announcement is made. "Mr. and Mrs. Shaw, your order is ready to be picked up at the meat counter."

"Go ahead." Mom flicks her hand at Dad.

The intercom crackles again. "Mrs. Shaw. You have a phone call."

Mom sighs. "Work is never finished."

They bustle away. As soon as they're gone, I hurry toward the checkout with the cart. I haven't finished my grocery list yet, but I am not chancing bumping into Mom and Dad again.

We check out without further incident. Once the groceries are in the trunk and we're on our way back to the bakery, the tension leaks out of my body.

Phew. Another confrontation with my parents is over and I survived. But then I notice the gleam in Jeremy's eyes. He has questions and I'm afraid he won't be as easily distracted as my parents.

Where's a kraken when you need one?

Chapter 21

"Trading trauma for truth. Classic negotiation strategy."

JEREMY

"Thank you for helping," Parker says once we've finished putting away the groceries in the kitchen.

She's cute if she thinks I'm leaving without learning what the fuck her parents were talking about.

She opens the door and tries to usher me outside. Totally cute. And not happening.

I cross my arms over my chest and lean against the table. "We can do this here or upstairs in the loft but it's happening."

"What's happening?" She fiddles with the hem of her t-shirt and refuses to meet my gaze.

I pinch her chin and lift her face. "Princess."

"I thought I was a queen."

"In the bakery, you're a queen. When it comes to the two of us, you're my naughty little princess."

Her eyes flare, and her mouth drops open. As much as I'd love to explore her mouth before moving on to other parts of her, I'm not letting this subject drop.

"Princess," I growl. "What the hell happened with your parents?"

She shuts down. The passion disappears from her eyes, and the hint of happiness is gone.

"None of your business. This relationship is only for the season. It doesn't give you access to all of my secrets."

"True." Agreeing this relationship is temporary has my stomach curling but I ignore it. I don't have more to offer Parker even if I wanted to.

"But while we're together, I won't allow anyone to treat you poorly. Not even your parents."

"I have an easy solution." If she says she wants to end this arrangement, I'm going to lose my shit. I'm not ready to end this. Not even close.

"What?" I bark.

"You can avoid going out in public with me. Easy peasy."

She looks extremely proud of herself. She's in for a wake-up call.

"I am not going to hide you away like you're my dirty little secret."

"Why not? This isn't serious."

My entire body rebels at the idea of us being some cheap temporary fling. I inhale a deep breath and get myself under control before I speak.

"I guess we're doing this here," I mutter.

She opens her mouth to argue with me but I slam a palm up. I'm done listening to her try and push me away.

"I told you I don't have contact with my parents." I wait for her to nod before I continue. "I didn't tell you why."

She places a hand on my chest. "You don't have to tell me, Scrooge."

I grasp her hand. "I'm telling you and then you're going to tell me everything that happened with your parents and culinary school."

She tries to yank her hand away but I hold fast. "I already told you everything."

I bend over until my face is inches from hers. "You did not tell me everything."

Surprise flashes in her bright blue eyes before she closes them.

"When I made my first million, I paid off my parents' debt – their house, credit cards, loans, all of it."

Her eyes fly open and she meets my gaze. "All of it? How much debt did they have?"

I snort. "Tons. Dad grew up rich. My great-grandfather founded an investment firm on Wall Street. There was money to burn. Until there wasn't."

Her brow wrinkles. "I don't understand."

"Instead of growing the business, dear old dad bled it dry. He wined and dined clients all over the world while not paying one bit of attention to their money. Once clients realized their portfolios were no longer growing, they moved to different investment firms."

Her nose wrinkles. "That sucks."

"No. What sucks is how my parents continued to live their lives as if their bank accounts were flush and the investment firm wasn't bankrupt."

"And so you paid off all of their debts."

I nod. "I did."

"I hear a but coming."

I blow out a breath. "When I paid off their debts, I warned them to start living within their means."

"But they didn't?"

"Nope. And they expect me to foot the bill when they fly off for breakfast in Paris. Or when Mom buys whatever bag is trendy. Or when they ski in Aspen. The list goes on and on."

Her jaw drops open. "You're supporting your parents?"

"No, I'm not."

"But—"

"And when I refused to pay their bills, they sued me."

"Sued you?"

"Yes, apparently, I owe them because they raised me."

She groans. "I know how that feels."

Which is exactly why I'm telling her this story I never tell anyone. Only Eli knows the truth about my parents because he was there. But I'm telling Parker to get her to open up to me.

"What happened with your parents?"

She blows out a breath. "You know the basics. My parents paid for culinary school, thinking I'd end up working in some fancy bakery in New York City or Paris. When I returned home to start this bakery instead, they became furious."

"Why?"

She scowls. "My parents are all about prestige. Having a child who owns a patisserie in Paris is prestigious. Having a daughter who owns *Pirate's Pastries* is not."

"Bullshit. You own and manage a bakery, Princess. You should be proud of yourself."

"Except I'm barely scraping by," she mutters.

I ignore the comment. I have bigger fish to fry. "Why aren't you working at a patisserie in Paris?"

She glares at me. "You sound like my parents."

"Who you are obviously lying to."

She gasps. "I'm not lying to them."

Lift a brow. "Really? And you didn't scratch your palm when you told your parents you don't know why you didn't get an apprenticeship after you finished culinary school?"

"I didn't…"

I point to her hand where she's scratching her palm.

"Neptune's beard," she mutters before stuffing her hands in her pockets.

I palm her neck and squeeze. "What happened, Princess?"

"Why do you think anything happened?"

"Because you're the best baker I've ever met and I've been to the best patisseries in Paris."

Her eyes light up. "You have? Was it heaven? What did you eat? Did it melt in your mouth? Was it orgasmic?"

I open my mouth to tell her I'll fly her to Paris some day for her to experience a patisserie for herself. I manage to bite my tongue before I say those words. I don't fly women to Paris. It creates expectations.

But I want to fly Parker to Paris. I want to witness the marvel on her face when she walks into a French patisserie for the first time. When she tries a madeleine for the first time.

"I'll give you a blow by blow of every patisserie I've ever visited in Paris if you tell me the truth."

"You're mean, Scrooge."

I brush the hair off her forehead. "I'm negotiating."

"But I've never told anyone what happened."

"I'll be your first."

"Ugh." She stomps her foot. "I never realized Scrooge was this tenacious."

"I can be very, very tenacious." I draw my finger down her face to her neck but stop before I touch her breasts. Her breath hitches.

"You're not playing fair."

"I never said I'd play fair, Princess."

She stares into my eyes for several moments before she nods. "Okay, I'll tell you. But if you ever tell anyone else, I will bake you a cake, the most delicious cake you've ever eaten, except it will be filled with a poison only Circe would know about. And you will die a slow, agonizing death while the doctors fail to diagnose you."

I shiver at the promise in her eyes. "Agreed."

"It's all Halston's fault."

"Halston sounds like a prick."

"Oh, he is." Her eyes narrow, and a muscle ticks in her jaw. "He's worse than a prick. He's a lying, conniving asshole who wouldn't know what to do with a rolling pin if it came with instructions."

I squeeze her hands. "What did he do?"

"At culinary school, not much. But when he found out I was graduating at the top of the class and therefore had secured the apprenticeship at a famous Paris patisserie, he lost his mind. He assumed since Daddy was rich, he'd get the spot. And he did."

"How?"

"He claimed I cheated on the final baking exam. He said I used bought caramel. As if I would ever buy caramel. The head chef didn't believe him. No one did. But the owner of the school insisted it was true – probably because Halston's dad was a billionaire who could buy anyone – and I lost my apprenticeship. It was too late in the year for me to apply for another one."

It all makes sense now. Why she's not in Paris. Why she hates billionaires. Why she wants nothing to do with my money.

"I could have waited a year for another chance but then I would have had to explain to my parents what happened." She shakes her head. "I'm never explaining to them how I thought Halston was a good guy. How I helped him at our final baking exam. How I thought he was different and cared for me. How I thought I loved him."

I growl. My princess did not love some entitled prick who used her.

"What's Halston's last name?"

She shakes a finger at me. "Nope. You aren't getting my revenge for me."

"I have connections. My revenge would target his parents and the little prick."

She fists her hands on her hips. "This is my problem to deal with. Not yours."

"Wrong. You're—"

My telephone rings to cut me off. Which is a good thing since I was about to say she's mine. Parker isn't mine. She's only mine for the season. On January first, I'll be gone from Smuggler's Hideaway and out of her life.

Chapter 22

"I'd flee my feelings faster if the damn door locked."

Parker

As soon as Jeremy steps away to answer his phone, I feel cold and alone. What did I do? Why did I confess my past to him? He's a billionaire who doesn't care about me. He's no one to me.

Except you're falling for him.

It doesn't matter what I feel. He isn't here to stay. And since he knows my pathetic story, he'll probably want to end our arrangement anyway. No one wants to be in a relationship with a loser. And I've got a bit fat L tattooed on my forehead.

I wring my hands as I try to figure out a way to erase my confession from Jeremy's brain. Or maybe rewind time. Why isn't there a sea creature who can bend time?

Oh, who am I kidding? There's no graceful way to exit this scenario. Fleeing it is.

I tiptoe out of the kitchen and close the door behind me as quietly as possible. I wait a moment for Jeremy's reaction but he's still talking on the phone. Time to get out of here.

I hurry down the street toward my apartment. I hope Annie's not home. I have no desire to argue with my roommate about her stealing my food today. I'm all argued out.

I barge into the apartment and blow out a breath in relief when Annie isn't lounging on the couch. I collapse on it and bury my face in my hands.

Why did I confess all my secrets to Jeremy? I've kept what happened at culinary school a secret for years. Why now? Why him?

Will he tell Eli what happened? Eli will tell Paisley and then the whole island will know what happened. Including my parents, who will not be amused.

If I ever have kids, I will never judge them. They can decide they want to dress up as sirens every day and sing on the street corner for their money and I won't judge them. I will love them. I'll also bring them food to eat and invite them over on holidays.

Because children deserve to be loved unconditionally. No matter what they do.

"Parker!" Jeremy shouts before he bangs on the door. "I know you're in there."

Screaming sirens in the sea. How does Jeremy know where I live?

I lower my voice and shout, "There ain't no Parker here."

"Parker," Jeremy growls. "I know this is your apartment."

I stomp to the door and fling it open. "How did you find my place? Did you use your 'connections'?"

He runs a hand through his hair. "I'm sorry. I never should have mentioned I have connections and will get revenge on Halston for you."

"You're forgiven." I try to shut the door but he pushes past me.

"Hey, I didn't invite you inside, Scrooge."

He studies the area and my cheeks heat in response. There's a reason no one's ever invited here. And it's not because Annie steals all my food.

"Why aren't there any decorations on your Christmas tree?"

"Annie ate them."

"Who's Annie? What..." He shakes his head. "Never mind. I've seen enough."

I motion to the door. "You can see yourself out."

"I'm not going anywhere without you."

Guess I'm not argued out after all. I plant my fists on my hips. "You are not ordering me around."

"You enjoy it when I order you around."

I hate how he's right. But he's not completely right. "Only when we're naked."

"I can make that happen but not here."

"You know where the door is."

He sighs. "Princess, this isn't scraping by. This is drowning." He reaches for me. "Come on. We're leaving."

"*We* aren't going anywhere. I'm staying here. I'm home."

"This isn't a home, Princess."

I growl. "Don't you dare call me princess."

"Why are you living here anyway?"

"I can live wherever the hell I want."

"If you can live wherever you want, why are you living in squalor?"

"In squalor?" I stab his chest with my finger. "You don't get to judge me. No one gets to judge me. This is my life and I'm doing the best I can."

"Bullshit."

"Bullshit? What do you mean bullshit?"

"I'm not an idiot."

"I never said you were."

"And I'm not blind."

"Maybe not, but I'm confused. Where are you going with this conversation?"

He squeezes my shoulder. "I saw how many Thanksgiving pies you baked. And I know how much you charged. The bakery is busy every day."

I shake my head. "Not as busy as it was before the chain coffee place opened on the promenade."

He dips his chin to concede my point. "Maybe not as busy, but it's still busy every day. And you sell out of your baked goods every single day."

"Maybe because I know what the demand is and don't want to waste food."

"Nope. There's something else going on. Where is the money going?"

I swallow. "What money?"

"The money you're earning from the bakery."

I realize I'm scratching my palm and fist my hand. "Shouldn't you know this? You own a business. I have operating costs – mortgage, utilities, personnel, supplies…"

He pinches my jaw. "You're earning more than enough to pay for your operating costs and live in a better place. Where is your money going?"

"How do you know what my operating costs are? Real estate on Smuggler's Hideaway is expensive. Especially on the main drag of Smuggler's Cove, where all the restaurants and shops are."

I stare into his eyes. *Believe me. Drop this.*

"Where is your money going?"

Damn it. Apparently, my ability to use mind control on others isn't as good as a siren's. I wonder if there are any sirens out there willing to give me lessons. Or is mind control a gift you can't learn?

"Why are you insistent on learning all of my secrets?"

"Because your secrets are holding you back."

Ugh. He couldn't give a controlling asshole answer I could ignore? He has to have a good answer? And he's not giving up.

I throw my arms in the air. "I'm saving money to pay my parents back for culinary school. There. Are you happy now?"

He growls. "No. I'm not fucking happy. Those people do not deserve your money."

I don't disagree. "Maybe if I pay them back, they'll stop complaining about how I wasted their money."

Maybe they'll love me again. And invite me to holiday meals. I don't say those things. It's pathetic to still yearn for your parents' love when they've made it perfectly clear how little regard they have for you. But here we are.

Jeremy wraps his arms around me and pulls me near. "Princess, your parents aren't worth your sacrifice."

"How do you know?"

"Because parents don't allow their daughter to live this way if they can help it."

"They don't know where I live."

He kisses my hair. "Yes, they do. Everyone in town knows you live here."

Shame fills me. "They do?"

"How do you think I found you?"

"Duh. You asked Eli."

"I didn't ask Eli. I asked at *Smuggler's Cove* and they couldn't tell me fast enough. Also, they want you to know Viking is doing well."

I latch onto the excuse to change the topic. "I miss my little Viking."

"If you didn't live here, you could have him with you all the time."

So much for my grand idea to change the subject. I push away from Jeremy. He holds strong to me for a second before dropping his arms.

I feel cold and lonely without his arms around me, but I ignore the feeling. I'll examine my emotions later. When I'm alone.

"Jeremy, I'm not moving. This is what I can afford."

"Because you're saving money to pay back your parents." I open my mouth to speak but he places a finger on my lips to stop me. "Your parents didn't loan you the money for your schooling, did they?" I shake my head. "Did they ask for the money back?" I shake my head again. "This is what parents do. They pay for their children's education to help them get started in the world."

"But I want to pay them back."

He blows out a breath. "I'm not going to change your mind on this, am I?"

"No, sorry."

He glances around the room and frowns. "I don't want to leave you here."

"I'll be fine."

"I don't like it."

I snort. "Welcome to real life. Not everything that happens will be to your liking."

"At least let me take you out to dinner."

My stomach rumbles in response.

"Did you eat lunch?"

My nose wrinkles. "Does a cookie count?"

"No. A cookie doesn't count." He offers me his hand. "Come on. Let me feed you."

I hesitate. Is he offering to feed me out of pity? I don't need anyone to pity me. Especially not a billionaire who can buy and sell this entire apartment building a million times over.

My stomach rumbles to remind me I'm hungry and there's no food in my apartment. If I want to eat, I'll have to leave anyway.

"Fine. But I'm choosing where we eat."

He grins. "I accept your conditions."

He places his hand on my lower back and ushers me out of the apartment. He frowns when we pass the broken elevator and the unlocked front door but he doesn't say anything.

I expected him to shove his wealth in my face. But he hasn't.

Come on, Jeremy. Be a little bit of a jerk before I fall head over heels in love with you. And you break my heart when you leave Smuggler's Hideaway for good.

Chapter 23

"I wanted control. She took the couch – and the lead."

JEREMY

"I can't believe there's a Chinese restaurant on Smuggler's Hideaway," I say as Parker dumps another serving of shrimp fried rice onto her plate.

When she suggested take-out, I saw it as the perfect opportunity to get her back in the loft. A place I don't intend her to ever leave.

I can't allow her to live in her apartment. Especially not when the reason she's living there is to save money to repay her parents, who are complete assholes.

"*Wok the Plank* has been a staple in Smuggler's Rest for about a decade. David and Ang moved here from San Francisco with their daughter, May, for her to train with Miles."

"Miles? As in Eli's younger brother?"

"Yep." She settles back on the sofa next to me. "Miles used to be a world-class surfer until he injured himself in Hawaii."

"Does May still surf?"

"She's the surf instructor at *Hideaway Haven Resort.*"

"Have you ever surfed?"

She snorts. "My parents are orthodontists. I've never engaged in any activity that might ruin my perfect teeth." She smiles to show off her teeth. "I blame Miles. He chipped his front tooth when a surfboard hit him in the face."

Jealousy flares to life in my stomach. Were Parker and Miles a couple? "Isn't Miles five years younger than you?"

"Seven. But who's counting?" She shrugs.

"Are you into younger men?"

She points at me with her chopsticks. "You're a year younger than me."

"So, yes, you are into younger men."

She rolls her eyes. "Who says I'm into you?"

I set my plate down on the coffee table before doing the same with hers.

"What are you doing? We haven't finished eating yet."

"Answering your challenge." I crawl over her until she's forced to lay down on the sofa.

Her breath quickens, but she doesn't give in. Not my princess. "I didn't challenge you."

"Sure, you did. And now I'm going to prove how into me you are."

She bites her bottom lip and looks up at me from beneath her lashes. "How?"

I rake my gaze over her body. "Where to begin?"

"I have an idea."

I lift my gaze to meet hers. "Which is?"

She hooks her leg around mine and rears up until I'm forced onto my back. She plants her hands on my chest and settles on my thighs.

"How about I'm in charge this time?"

I growl. "I'm in charge in the bedroom."

"Good thing we're not in the bedroom then."

"This is a loft. The entire room is a bedroom."

"Agree to disagree." She wiggles on top of me and my cock responds by lengthening and hardening. "Something agrees with me," she mutters before squeezing me over my jeans.

I moan. "You're sitting on top of me and I have a perfect view of your breasts. Of course, I'm hard."

She giggles before jiggling her breasts. "Do you mean these?"

I slap her hands out of the way. "Those are mine to play with."

"I'll let you play with mine if I can play with yours."

I squeeze her nipples. "What exactly are you suggesting?"

She leans over until she can whisper into my ear. "I ride you until you see stars."

My cock pulses in my jeans. It wants Parker to ride me while she's naked and her breasts are free and bouncing.

My fingers dig into her hips. "I prefer to be in charge."

She sits up and shrugs. "I can ride you until I get off and then you can be in charge."

I don't usually negotiate with women in the bedroom. But I can't seem to stop myself from giving Parker whatever she wants.

"Clothes off," I order.

She whips off her sweater. "I'm getting naked because I want to. Not because you ordered me to."

She can say what she wants. I saw the way her eyes flared when I ordered her to strip. I know she gets off on me being in charge.

But apparently, she has a point to prove today. And after all the secrets she revealed to me this afternoon – secrets painful for her to confess to – I'm loath to deny her. She needs to feel as if she has some control in this relationship and she can have what she wants. For a little while.

I tap her thigh. "All of your clothes off."

"Scrooge is bossy." She rolls her eyes but stands to do my bidding. She shoves her jeans down her legs revealing her panties.

She starts to climb back on me but I stop her. "Bra and panties are clothing, too."

She stares at me for a long moment before nodding. She removes both items and now she's standing before me – gloriously naked with all of her curves on display. Curves, I can't wait to get my hands and mouth on again. And I will.

She opens up her arms. "Do I meet with your approval?"

"More than," I growl. "You're fucking perfect."

"I'm not perfect. My thighs are too thick. My hips are too wide. My breasts are too big."

"You're perfect to me." With a start, I realize I'm not lying to get what I want. She seriously is perfect for me.

Shit. I'm falling for this small town baker. I never saw her coming, but she blasted straight through my defenses.

I grit my teeth. I may be falling for her but nothing will come of it. I've learned my lesson about relationships since I've become a billionaire. My parents aren't the only people who tried to take advantage of me.

"Condom." I motion toward the nightstand.

She contemplates me for a moment before making her way to the bed and opening the drawer. She snatches a foil package before returning to me. I watch her naked body as she moves. I could watch her all day.

My cock disagrees. It wants to be buried deep in her body. And I can't do that if I'm staring at her moving around.

She places the condom on the coffee table before climbing on me. Her core is nestled against my cock. I can feel her heat through my jeans.

I don't want to wait. I want to pound into her pussy. But I grit my teeth and stay still. Parker's in charge. For now.

Her mouth melds to mine and I groan as her taste hits me – coffee, sugar, and a hint of sea. I love the taste of her. I want to drown in it. I'll probably get hard every time I sniff the ocean in the future but I don't care. She's worth it.

She opens for me and I dive into her mouth. I explore her mouth as if I can't get enough. Because I can't. Kissing is usually foreplay I'm forced to do before the main act. But not with Parker. I could kiss her all day.

She drags her fingernails along my unshaven jaw as I massage and knead her breasts while she grinds down on my cock until it weeps.

I grunt and yank my mouth away from hers. "This is going to be over awful quick if you don't stop grinding down on me."

She bats her eyelashes at me. "I thought I was in charge."

"Just warning you, I can't fuck you if I come in my jeans like a damn teenager."

She bursts into laughter. Her head falls back and her breasts bounce as she laughs. I'll give her a reason to stop laughing.

I pinch her nipples and twist. Hard. She gasps as she grounds down on my cock again.

"Condom," I order.

She snatches it from the table before scooting down my legs. She snaps my jeans open but I shackle her wrists.

"Careful."

She blows out a breath before nodding. I release her and she draws the zipper down so slowly, I have to grit my teeth before I take over from her. This is her show.

Once my jeans are open, she digs into my underwear and pulls my cock out. "Put the condom on me."

Even from underneath, I'm in command. Guiding her hands as she rolls the condom over my cock, slow enough to drive me insane. When she's finished, she perches above me.

"Put me inside you," I grumble.

She sinks down on me and I inhale a deep breath before I grasp her hips and take charge. Before I start thrusting into her from below.

She bottoms out and gasps.

"Are you okay? Are you hurt?"

She bobs her head.

"Say the words, Princess."

"I'm not hurt. I need a second to adjust, is all."

I'll give her something else to think about. I sneak a hand in between our bodies to touch her clit. I rub the little nub until Parker's head falls back and she starts to lift and lower herself on me. Once she's found her rhythm, I abandon her clit for her hips.

"Lean over. I want to suck on those pretty nipples while you ride me."

She plants her hands on my chest and I latch onto a nipple. I suck and bite and nibble until her movements become erratic. Then, I take over.

I use my hands on her hips to raise and lower her on my cock while I thrust up into her. Her walls tighten and convulse around my cock until I have to force my way inside.

"Are you going to come for me, Princess?"

"Uh huh."

"Are you going to scream my name when you come all over my cock?"

"Nuh uh."

She's cute. I'll make her scream. I keep one hand on her hip to guide her while sneaking the other hand between us. I barely touch her clit before she explodes.

"Oh god. Oh god."

"Not god," I growl. "Jeremy."

"Jeremy," she breathes out as she rides out her orgasm.

I flip us over until I'm on top and her legs are wrapped around me. I pound into her until my orgasm hits.

"Parker," I growl as I come.

I continue to pump into her until I'm completely spent. I collapse on top of her before rolling us to our sides. We barely fit on the sofa but I'm too exhausted to move.

Sex with Parker is better than anything I've ever felt before. Is this how it feels when you fall for someone?

I force those thoughts away. This is temporary. I don't have anything more to offer.

Chapter 24

"Apparently, saltwater taffy is a terrible defense strategy."

PARKER

I snuggle into the warmth of Jeremy. I could wake up this way every single morning. After a night of exploring each other's bodies. It would be easy to get used to.

No, no, no, I can't get used to waking up in Jeremy's arms. Our relationship has an expiration date. And it's coming up soon.

On the first of January, I will be officially dumped. Does it count as dumped when the date was agreed upon in advance?

My heart doesn't care. It's dreading the heartbreak. My heart is a big, fat drama queen.

There will be no heartbreak. Because I am not going to fall in love with Jeremy. I may be halfway there but I can stop this fall. I'll simply encase my heart in saltwater taffy that's been hardened too much after cooling. No one can chew through hardened saltwater taffy.

Jeremy's arm tightens around my waist before he kisses my shoulder. "Good morning, Princess."

My breath hitches at the feel of his lips on my skin. I remember how good it felt when he rained kisses all over my body. Stop the fall, Parker. Stop the fall.

"I still maintain I'm a queen."

He chuckles and since his body is pressed up against mine, I feel the vibrations throughout my body. Heart. Saltwater taffy. No chewing.

"You can be a queen, but you're my princess."

His princess? I want to be his princess. And not only until New Year's Day.

"I should probably get going," I say, since this whole heart encased in saltwater taffy is not working.

He clears his throat. "We should talk."

My stomach drops. Scuttle my cookies. Is he breaking up with me now? I still have a few weeks. I'm not ready to say goodbye. I'm afraid I'll never be ready to say goodbye.

"I'm not apologizing for the soy sauce."

His fingers dig into my hip. "It's your fault there's soy sauce all over the sheets."

"Disagree. If you hadn't attacked me while I was eating, there wouldn't be soy sauce on the sheets."

"You said you could eat while I explored your body."

I roll around to face him. "You didn't say explore my body. You said tickle me."

"Same thing."

"It is not the same thing! You yanked open my legs and started to taste me."

Tickling, I can handle. I'm not ticklish. For the most part. Having a man give me pleasure while I'm eating? That I apparently can't handle.

"Hmm…" His eyes flare. "Good idea."

My nipples pebble at the promise in his voice.

"But we need to talk first."

I groan. "You're ruining morning sex."

"We'll have sex in a moment."

I seriously doubt we'll have sex in a moment if he tells me this arrangement is finished. I'll be hiding in the bathroom crying instead. Crap on a mermaid's tail. My eyes are already welling with tears.

"What do you want to talk about?" Might as well get this over with.

"You shouldn't be living in that hellhole you refer to as an apartment."

Relief hits me. He isn't ending this affair early. But then I realize what he said.

I glare at him. "You don't get to tell me what to do."

"I can't believe you're fighting me on this."

I rear back. "You can't? Are you so used to bulldozing over people's wishes that the idea someone doesn't jump to do your bidding is foreign?"

"I'm not bulldozing over your wishes."

I raise an eyebrow. "Really? You're not telling me where to live?"

"This is ridiculous. You can't possibly want to live in your crappy apartment."

I don't. But I'm not admitting to anything. I am not giving him any fuel for his argument.

"Not all of us are rich snobs who refuse to live somewhere because it's not a penthouse."

A muscle ticks in his jaw, but to his credit, he doesn't lash out at me. He inhales a deep breath and forces himself to calm down. Which doesn't make me fall for him more. Nope. Not me. Heart encased in hardened salt water taffy over here.

"Why don't you stay here in this loft?"

My heart stutters in my chest. "With you?"

"I'll go stay with Eli."

Calm down, heart. He isn't asking me to move in with him. Which isn't disappointing. Not at all.

"I thought you couldn't work at Eli's house. It's why you wanted to stay here in the first place."

"I'll figure it out."

"No." I shake my head. "I can't allow it."

The corners of his lips tip up in an almost smile. "Allow it? You're going to tell me what I can and can't do?"

"Yep. I'm the boss here. Haven't you noticed?"

He growls. "I'm in charge in the bedroom. And guess where we are?"

I roll my eyes. "You're only in charge in the bedroom when it's naked time."

His gaze rakes over my body. "Good thing you're naked."

I wag my finger at him. "But it's not naked time."

"It's not?" He presses his cock into my stomach.

I scoot away out of his reach. "You're not using sex to convince me to move in here."

He sighs. "Can't you be reasonable?"

I narrow my eyes at him. "Are you saying I'm unreasonable because I'm a woman?"

"No, I'm saying you're unreasonable because you're being stubborn as shit. This place is paid for until January first. You can stay here by yourself and still save money for your shitty parents who don't deserve a dime from you."

I flinch.

"Fuck. I'm sorry. I shouldn't have said your parents are shitty. It's true, but I shouldn't have said it."

"You're crap at apologizing."

He shrugs. "I'm being honest. You're working yourself to death to pay your parents back for your education when they won't even frequent your bakery."

I drop my chin to my chest. "I know."

"Hey." He pinches my chin and lifts my head to meet his gaze. "I truly am sorry. I know how it feels to have shitty parents."

"I'm trying to improve the situation."

He smiles but it's not a happy smile to show off his dimples. "Here's the thing, Princess. You can't improve the situation on your own. Your relationship with your parents won't improve unless they want it to as well."

"I know," I mutter.

But maybe it will help if I pay them back the money they spent on my culinary school. Maybe they'll be proud and stunned and amazed by how much money it is.

Jeremy sighs. "I'm going to move into Eli's house no matter what."

"You can't work at Eli's house, and you have a deadline." I don't know what the deadline is. He's been very secretive about it, but I know there is one.

He grins and this time his dimples come out to play. "It'll be fine. I've been inspired recently."

"I'm your muse."

"You're my muse."

"I take payment in orgasms."

He smirks. "And I gladly deliver."

I squirm. "Get to delivering."

"First, you need to promise you'll move into this loft for as long as I've paid the rent."

I roll my eyes. "Fine. I'll move in."

Christmas is just over a week away. I'll be spending all of my time at the bakery anyway. Whether I sleep two hours here or two hours at my apartment doesn't matter at this point.

"For as long as I've paid the rent?"

"You're worse than a mermaid with a pirate on her line."

He ignores me and repeats, "For as long as I've paid the rent?"

"Fine. Fine. For as long as you've paid the rent. Now will you ravish me and give me orgasms?"

"On your back," he grumbles.

I shiver at the promise in his voice. Yes, please. I roll onto my back and he snatches the sheet away from me.

He gazes down at me with adoration in his eyes. No, not adoration. Jeremy doesn't adore me. This is simply a mutual agreement to satisfy our sexual urges until he leaves the island. Nothing more. Nothing less.

"Hands on the headboard."

"Yes, sir. Right away, sir."

He narrows his eyes at me. "Quiet or I'll gag you."

"No gagging. Handcuffs and blindfolds are okay. But gagging is not."

He smirks. "I'll have to rustle up some handcuffs."

If he expects me to protest, he'll be waiting a long time. I've discovered a new side of my sexuality with Jeremy. And this side enjoys being tied up. If the tying up is being done by him.

Jeremy kisses his way up my leg and I forget all about my fear of getting my heart broken. It's impossible to think when he concentrates on me and my body.

And I wouldn't want it any other way.

Chapter 25

"Who needs treasure when you've got cookies and chaos?"

JEREMY

I whistle as I walk down the stairs in Eli's house toward the kitchen for some coffee.

"Someone's happy this morning," Eli grumbles from where he's laying with his head on the kitchen table.

"I nearly finished the *Synq* app."

His head whips up from the table. "You did?"

"He's obviously been inspired," Paisley says as she sweeps into the room with a sleeping Stephanie in her arms.

"Enough with your matchmaking."

She grins. "But it's obviously working."

"There's no future for me with Parker. As soon as the New Year arrives, I'm leaving Smuggler's Hideaway."

Acid builds in my stomach at those words but I ignore it. Relationships aren't for me. Not even with the woman I'm falling for.

She scowls. "You don't have to leave. Eli lives here and he's your CFO for *Apparoo*."

"He doesn't need to be in California to be the numbers man. I'm the CEO and head developer. I need to be there to run my team."

She shrugs. "Move *Apparoo* to the island."

Not a bad idea. I could see Parker whenever I want. Watch Stephanie grow up. Hang out with my best friend. All while I'm far away from gold diggers.

I shake my head. It's an impossible dream. "Move a multi-billion dollar company across the country? Sure. Why not? I'll snap my fingers and make it happen."

She rolls her eyes. "You're Jeremy Holland. You can make anything happen."

Eli growls. "No flirting with my best friend."

Paisley's brow wrinkles. "I wasn't flirting."

"It was flirting."

I let them argue. I know where I can find better coffee anyway.

When I arrive at *Pirate's Pastries* fifteen minutes later, the place is packed. I manage to push my way through the crowd to Parker.

"What is happening?" I ask after I kiss her on her cheek.

"It's the *Mermaid Treasure Hunt*," she squeals.

My brow wrinkles. "I thought you weren't participating."

She beams up at me. "I won the gingerbread house contest. I used the prize money to pay for the moonshine."

Damn. I wanted to pay for the moonshine. But she was adamant about not participating in the treasure hunt. My stubborn little princess is a pain in my ass sometimes.

"Parker!"

"Sorry. Cindy needs me."

She starts to rush away but I shackle her wrist to stop her. "How can I help?"

"Are you sure?"

I growl. I don't deign to answer her question. She's my princess. Of course, I'm helping. "What can I do?"

She drags me into the kitchen. My eyes widen at the sight. There are trays of cookies on every single surface. It's only been two days since I last saw her. How did she do all this baking in the meantime?

She points to the parchment paper. "Each sea salt caramel coin cookie needs to be wrapped and a small scroll affixed to the top of the package."

I pick up a scroll and unroll it. "Not all treasure is hidden. Some is baked," I read out loud.

"It matches the clue to find this spot on the treasure map. *Golden coins and hidden loot, follow the scent of something sweet and cute. A pirate's prize, a mermaid's treat – Where sugar and sass and sea salt meet.*"

The clue is perfect. It points players to *Pirate's Pastries* without naming it directly and is on brand.

"I should hire the Smuggler's Hideaway tourist council for my marketing team."

"Too bad no one on the council would move away from Smuggler's Hideaway. Not even for the outrageous salaries you probably pay."

If I moved *Apparoo* to the island, it wouldn't be a problem. I stop those thoughts before I get carried away. No one's moving to the island. Parker and I are together only for the season. Once the season is over, we're over.

My gut rolls at the thought but I ignore it. I know better than to get attached to a woman. Even if the woman in question refused my help and managed to figure out a way to do what she wanted anyway. I can't help but admire Parker.

"Parker!"

"I really need to go." She pushes up on her toes to kiss me. "Don't eat too many of the cookies."

I'm not going to eat any cookies. Except when I notice the cookies are in the shape of old pirate coins and drizzled with sea salt caramel with a shimmer of edible gold dust, I can't resist. She didn't forbid me to eat any after all.

I stuff one into my mouth and moan as the flavor of shortbread and sea salt caramel melts in my mouth. Parker is a genius when it comes to baking.

I package cookies and attach small scrolls to the packages until my back aches. I moan as I stretch. I don't know how Parker does this every day. She really is a princess.

"Put it down!" Parker screams.

At her shout, I run into the café. A man has a gingerbread house lifted in the air. Parker is glaring at him.

"I found it! It's my treasure," the man slurs.

I make my way to Parker and shove her behind me. Drunken men can't be trusted and nothing will happen to Parker on my watch.

"Put down the gingerbread house," I order the man.

"No. It's mine."

"It's not yours. It's Parker's." And no one steals from Parker. No one.

"Nuh uh. It's the final treasure. I won the Mermaid Treasure Hunt."

Parker tries to push past me but I block her. She's mine to protect. And I will protect her. From drunken guests, asshole parents, whoever threatens her will deal with me.

"There is no final treasure," Parker says. "And you can't win the treasure hunt."

"What's the porpoise of a treasure hunt if there's no winner?"

"Porpoise? I think you mean purpose."

"Whatever." He dismisses me with a wave of his hand and the gingerbread house nearly goes crashing to the floor.

"Unless you want your treasure hunt to end in the ER, put the gingerbread house down."

"Is the ER on the treasure map?"

He looks back at his crew and sways. The gingerbread house tilts toward the floor. No one is dropping Parker's hard work on my watch. I snatch the gingerbread house from him.

"Hey! You stole my prize."

I pass the gingerbread house to Parker before confronting the drunk again. I stalk forward and he's forced to back up until he's at the door to the bakery.

"You will leave this bakery and not come back until you're sober, do you understand me?"

He stares up at me with his mouth hanging open.

"Unless you want to visit the ER for real."

Someone from his group grabs his arm and pulls him away. "We got it."

I follow them outside and watch until they're out of sight. Only then does my heart rate slow down to normal. I can't handle the thought of Parker being threatened or her not being safe.

I've never been protective of a woman before but Parker isn't any woman. She isn't spending her days dropping thousands of dollars on shoes she'll only wear once. Or wasting hours scrolling on social media.

She works hard and she doesn't want my money. She wants to do it all on her own. I couldn't admire her more.

"I knew you loved snow," Parker says as she wraps her arms around me from behind.

"What?"

She giggles as she motions to the sky. "It's snowing. It's why you're standing outside, isn't it?"

"Yep. I love snow."

I'm obviously lying, but she doesn't call me on it.

"Too bad it'll be gone in a few hours. The snow never lasts long on Smuggler's Hideaway. Except for last year. We had this big snowstorm. They had to cancel the treasure hunt. Although some people decided they could bike in the snow anyway." She laughs. "They couldn't."

I spin around and envelop her in my arms. "Have you always loved snow?"

"Yeah." Her sigh is wistful. "When I was young, my parents and I would go skiing for a week in the winter. Until they realized I preferred to lounge by the big fireplace in the cabin with a book and a hot cocoa while they skied. When I stopped skiing, they went without me."

I scowl. "They went without you?"

"It was okay. The previous owner of *Pirate's Pastries* would watch over me for the week. Alice taught me how to make sugar cookies and frosting, and hot cocoa."

"Where's Alice now?"

Pain fills her bright blue eyes. "She died two years after I bought the bakery from her. Breast cancer."

I squeeze her. "I'm sorry."

"Don't be." She glances up at me, tears glistening in her eyes. "Alice was ready to go. Her husband was gone and most of her friends had gone as well. It was her time."

"I can still be sorry you miss her."

She sighs. "I do. She taught me everything I know about baking."

I'm glad Parker had Alice in her life. Alice was probably more of a mother figure than her real mom, who went skiing without her. Her parents are assholes.

She taps my mouth. "No scowling when we're standing outside in the snow." She buries her face in my shoulder. "Today was a good day."

"Yea?"

"I introduced thousands of people to my cookies. I watched my temporary boyfriend go all territorial on me. And now it's snowing. What more could a woman want?"

I tip her chin up. "How about we go warm up with some of your famous hot chocolate?"

Her eyes sparkle. "I have some moonshine leftover."

"Lead the way, Princess."

I follow her into the bakery with a grin on my face. Smuggler's Hideaway is magical. I wouldn't mind living here.

The thought should scare me. But it doesn't.

Nothing can scare me when I'm holding hands with Parker. Including the thought of moving my company across the country.

Chapter 26

"The price of betrayal? Twelve months of rent. Apparently."

PARKER

"Hey, Jerry."

"You sound happy."

Well, let me see. I won the gingerbread house contest. I had a ball hosting a stop at the Mermaid Treasure Hunt. And I spent the night wrapped up in a sexy billionaire who – I pat the cold sheets next to me – apparently left in the middle of the night.

"What's up?" I ask my accountant instead of telling him my life story. He'll hear from the gossip train soon enough – if he hasn't already.

"There's a weird transaction in your bank account."

I groan. "Don't tell me I have to pay a ton of taxes on my winnings from the gingerbread contest. I already spent the money on moonshine."

Words to live by. Don't spend your money on moonshine in case the tax man comes calling.

"No worry there. Congratulations on your win, by the way."

"Thank you."

"There's another transaction here I can't figure out. It's a large deposit."

"How large of a deposit?"

"Twelve months of rent on the loft above the bakery. Give or take."

Twelve months of rent on the loft? Who would…. Drowning pirates in the stormy sea! I should have known Jeremy was up to something when he made me promise to stay in the loft for as long as the rent is paid.

"I'm going to kill him."

"Excuse me?"

"Not you, Jerry. You're safe."

"What do you want me to do about this transaction?"

"Can you return the money?"

"I don't have a bank account number to return it to."

I flip the covers off and jump out of bed. "I'll get you the number."

I end the call and immediately dial Jeremy's number. He doesn't answer. Of course, he doesn't. He's probably hiding from me.

He thinks he can hide from me? He thinks wrong. I will show him.

But then I notice the time on the clock. I need to start baking. I will show him. After the morning baking is done.

I'm elbow deep in brioche dough when the back door to the kitchen opens. I don't need to look to know Jeremy has arrived. His sandalwood scent gives him away.

"Let me get this bread in the oven and then we'll talk."

"Shit." He rubs a hand over his unshaved jaw. "You found out."

"Yes, I found out. Even people who live on Podunk islands have accountants."

"I've apologized for the Podunk comment."

"Apologizing doesn't mean I forgot."

I stab a finger at him. Unfortunately, I'm holding a pastry brush which is loaded with melted butter. Melted butter flies everywhere. In my face. In my hair. On my table. Naturally, it doesn't touch Jeremy. Mr. Untouchable Billionaire who enjoys throwing his money around.

The door to the café swings open.

"Did you…" Cindy trails off when she notices Jeremy. She glares at him. "What did you do?"

"Cindy. Please return to the café."

"No. If this asshole hurt you, I won't stand for it."

My eyes widen. Cindy is twenty years old, shorter than me, and weighs half what I do. And yet she's standing here glaring at Jeremy as if she's ready to rumble.

He holds up his hands. "I didn't hurt her."

Cindy ignores him and raises an eyebrow at me.

"He's an idiot, but he didn't hurt me."

"There are more ways to hurt a person than physically."

Judging by the look on her face, she knows this from personal experience. I don't know her well – she's merely filling in for Holly this morning – but it's time I had a sit-down with her.

"I appreciate your concern, Cindy. I promise you. Jeremy didn't hurt me physically or mentally. He's merely an idiot."

She studies me for a moment before nodding. "Fine. But if I hear yelling, I'm calling the police."

"What happened to her?" Jeremy asks once she's gone.

"I don't know, but I'll find out."

"Let me know if I need to bang any heads together."

As if he'll be around. I finish brushing the dough with egg wash, place the tin in the oven, and set the timer for thirty minutes.

"Now." I whirl around and plant my hands on my hips. "Where were we?"

Jeremy opens his mouth to answer but I hold up a hand to stop him.

"I remember. It's time for me to rip you a new asshole for paying a year's rent on the loft."

He cringes. "I just…"

I wag my finger at him. "Tut. Tut. Tut. It's not your turn to speak yet. You spoke loud enough when you deposited the money without telling me. After procuring a promise from me to stay in the loft as long as you'd paid the rent. Knowing full well I would never make such a promise if I knew you'd paid for a year."

"I can't stand you living in that hellhole of an apartment."

"Too bad." I slap the empty tins on the table. "It's not your choice where I live." I pound my chest. "It's mine. It's my choice to save money to pay my parents back. It's my choice to rent out the loft to earn more income. My. Choice."

"But I have the money."

I growl. An honest to goodness growl. "You can't buy me with your money. I don't want anything to do with your money."

"Tell me about it," he mutters.

He's being facetious but I decide to let him have it.

"I didn't have sex with you because you're a billionaire. In fact, I'd prefer it if you didn't have money. It would make things easier. Such as when you decide you can buy my love. I'm not for sale."

"What do you want?" He bursts out. "This is how things work in my world."

I rear back. "In your world? You live in the same world as mine. The rules of love and trust, and friendship don't change because of money."

He snorts. "Wrong."

I cross my arms over my chest. "I'm wrong? Explain how I'm wrong."

"Women want one thing from me. They want my money. Why do you think I don't do relationships? Because every woman I think is different – every woman I hope won't be a gold digger – turns out the same way. They want me for my money."

"You have got to be kidding me," I grumble.

"This isn't a joke. This is how women treat me."

"And you thought I was the same as those gold diggers? You thought I'm some poor baker who would be happy to accept your money after a couple of tumbles in the hay."

He cringes. "Not exactly."

"Have I once asked for your money?"

"No."

"What happened when I refused your help to purchase the moonshine for the *Mermaid Treasure Hunt*?" I don't give him a chance to answer. "I'll tell you what happened. I figured out a way to pay for it by myself." I slap a hand on my chest. "Me. The poor little baker from the Podunk island figured it all out by herself. No big fancy billionaire needed. Thank you very much."

"I wanted to help."

"Do you need your ears cleaned out? Is there too much wax in there? Because you are not hearing me. Let me spell it out for you. I, Parker Shaw, owner of *Pirate's Pastries* and resident of Smuggler's Hideaway, do not need you, Jeremy Holland, billionaire tech developer of *Apparoo* fame, to come and save me. I can save myself."

He steps closer and reaches for me. I retreat. If he touches me now, there's no telling what I'll do to him. Break his fingers. Pour hot, melted butter over his head. Kiss him breathless. There are options galore.

"I'm sorry. I only tried to help."

I shake my head. "You don't see it."

"See what?"

"You did exactly what your parents and all those 'girlfriends' wanted you to do."

"Explain yourself," he grumbles.

"They want more than your money. They want you to give it to them without having to ask for it. They want you to rain gifts down on them. Spoiler alert. I don't give a shit about your money."

I make my way toward the café. I can't be in the presence of someone who thinks I can be bought any longer.

I stop with my hand on the door. "Let Eli know what bank account I can return the money to. He knows my accountant."

"Let Eli?"

"I'm sorry, Jeremy, but I can't be in the same room with you now. I'm fantasizing about hitting you with my rolling pin and we both know I wouldn't last in jail. They don't supply chocolate."

"I'll let Eli know."

"Thank you."

I hurry through the door to the café. Cindy calls out my name but I keep going. I need to be somewhere private before I break down.

The man I'm falling in love with doesn't understand me at all. I've had a lifetime of my parents not understanding me. I can't be with someone who doesn't get me. No matter how much my heart yearns for him. I can't do it.

Chapter 27

*"I developed an app into a billion-dollar business.
How hard can baking a cake be?"*

JEREMY

I pace the guest bedroom in Eli's mansion as I try to figure out what the hell to do. I really fucked up. I treated Parker like a gold digger when she's the farthest thing from one.

I pick up the phone to ring her to apologize but what good is a phone call going to do? I fling the phone on the bed and resume my pacing.

I need to apologize to Parker. This relationship has an expiration date, but I'm not ready to say goodbye to her. Not yet. I want to spend as much time with her as possible until I leave Smuggler's Hideaway.

The phone rings and I rush toward it. *Miranda calling.*

Women like Miranda are the reason I'm in this mess to begin with. I treated Parker the way those women want to be treated.

But not Parker. She doesn't care about money. She cares about this island, her community, her friends, baked goods, and chocolate.

Chocolate! That's it!

I'll buy her a cake. No. Buying a cake isn't enough. I'll bake her an apology cake. How hard can it be?

I check my watch. The bakery should be closed now. I still have the key to the back door. I can sneak into the kitchen and bake Parker a cake. When she arrives in the morning and sees it, she'll rush to forgive me.

Thirty minutes later, I'm in the bakery googling a chocolate cake recipe. I choose one with only three steps. I've got this.

I dig around in Parker's pantry. Once I've gathered all of the ingredients I need, I grab a bowl and get started.

I throw all of the dry ingredients into the bowl and mix them. This is easy.

I read the recipe, *add the eggs, vanilla, and oil. Mix for two minutes on medium speed with an electric mixer.*

Electric mixer. Electric mixer. Where is Parker's electric mixer?

There's a mixer with a bowl attached on the table but I already have a bowl. And, honestly, the machine appears a bit complicated.

I search her cupboard and come up with a hand mixer. Perfect.

I place the mixer in the bowl, switch it on, and bam! Flour flies everywhere. Shit. I switch it off and swipe a hand over my face, which is now covered in flour.

Easy cake recipe, my ass.

I gather up as much flour from the table as possible and add it back to the bowl. I mix the ingredients with a spoon. Once

I'm confident there's no dry flour to attack me anymore, I use the electric mixer to finish mixing the ingredients.

The recipe said to mix for two minutes but after two minutes, I notice the mixture is still lumpy. I decide to double the mixing time.

Now, we're getting somewhere.

Pour the batter into a pan.

Oh, right. I need a pan. I scan the room. There are pans everywhere. Of every shape and size. What size do I need?

I re-read the recipe but it doesn't mention anything about a pan size. I shrug. I guess it doesn't matter. I pour the batter into a sheet pan.

Wait. The recipe said 'prepared' pan. What does 'prepared' mean?

Grease and flour the pan. Uh oh. I skipped that line.

Oh well. The batter is in the pan now. I slide the pan into the oven.

There. All I need to do now is clean up and Parker will arrive tomorrow morning to a wonderful surprise. And then she'll forgive me. I hope.

The door bangs open and Parker stomps inside. "What in the name of the mermaids in the sea is happening here?"

I gesture to the oven. "Isn't it obvious?"

"Obvious?" She lifts a brow. "The oven isn't on."

"Shit. The recipe didn't say to switch on the oven."

"Really? There wasn't any mention of pre-heating the oven."

"Preheat? You have to preheat the oven?"

She marches to the oven and peers inside. She flinches at the view before clearing her throat. "If you don't preheat the oven, the cake will bake unevenly."

"Okay. Let me remove the cake and preheat the oven."

"There's no need."

"No need?"

She points to the oven. "Whatever *that* is should probably be thrown away."

I scowl. "It's cake batter. I mixed it myself."

"That much is obvious," she mutters before raising her voice. "If you need a cake, I'll bake you one in the morning."

"I don't want you to bake me a cake. I want to bake you a cake."

"But I'm a baker."

"Who loves chocolate." She blinks in confusion at me and I sigh. "I'm trying to apologize."

"With lumpy, uncooked chocolate cake batter?"

"It's not lumpy. I mixed it for twice as long as the recipe said to ensure there were no lumps."

She shivers. "Twice as long? We're definitely throwing the batter away."

I cross my arms over my chest. "What's wrong with mixing twice as long?"

"Overmixing the batter causes it to develop too much gluten, which creates a tough, dense cake."

"This is not working out the way I intended." I run a hand through my hair and Parker giggles.

"You have flour in your hair."

"You could have pretended not to notice," I mutter.

"And miss how adorably grumpy you are when I mention it?"

Adorably grumpy? Is she softening toward me? "Do you forgive me?"

Her nose wrinkles. "You haven't apologized yet."

I blow out a breath. "Parker Shaw, I'm sorry I paid for a year of rent for the loft."

"And you're sorry because?" She motions for me to continue.

"You don't need my money, and you can save your damn self?"

She studies me for a long moment. "Good enough."

I inch closer to her. When she doesn't back away, I dare to close in on her until I can see the little flecks of gray in her blue eyes.

"I really am sorry, Parker. I shouldn't have paid the rent, but I hate the idea of your suffering."

"My apartment isn't that bad."

"Do you want me to list all the reasons your apartment should be condemned?"

She grunts. "No."

I palm her neck. "I know I was an asshole who treated you like a money grubbing gold digger, but I want to resume our arrangement."

"An affair until you leave the island?"

My stomach clenches. New Year's Day is less than two weeks away. I can't imagine saying goodbye to Parker in two weeks. But I don't know what else I have to offer her. I've never managed to have a healthy relationship.

"What about more?" I ask before I can overthink the situation.

"More?" She narrows her eyes at me. "What does more mean?"

"Honestly, I have no clue. I just know I don't want to say goodbye to you."

She stares up at me from beneath her lashes. "You don't?"

I squeeze her neck. "I don't. You intrigue me, Parker."

"Because I threw your money in your face?"

"And you're sweet and funny and have a strange obsession with mermaids and have an otter for a pet and smell of chocolate and taste like coffee and sugar. You have curves I can't get enough of, and I love the way you let me lead in the bedroom."

She frowns. "I don't let you lead in the bedroom."

I lift a brow.

"Not all the time."

I nod to concede her point.

"What do you say? Do you want to try 'more' with me?"

She nibbles on her bottom lip. "How will this work? I live in Smuggler's Hideaway. You live on the other side of the country."

I shrug. "I also own a private jet."

She rolls her eyes. "You had to bring up your jet."

"What's the purpose of being wealthy if I don't have a jet to mitigate the negative consequences of a long-distance relationship?"

"You make a good point."

"Does this mean you agree to more?"

She blows out a breath. "I'll probably regret this but yes, I agree to more, whatever more means."

"We'll figure it out," I murmur before my lips find hers. She sighs and I sweep my tongue into her mouth. Her taste of coffee, sugar, and a hint of sea hits me and I groan. I'm addicted to the flavor. I won't ever get enough. I don't want to ever get enough.

I wrap my arms around her and press her against the table. It wobbles and something crashes to the floor. I tear my lips from hers before nibbling along her jaw to her ear.

"Shall we take this upstairs before we're both covered in flour?"

She laughs and motions to the mixing bowl on the floor. "Are you afraid of a little flour?"

"Make fun of me, will you?" I play growl before lifting her up and throwing her over my shoulder. "My princess needs to be reminded of who's in charge."

She giggles as I carry her out of the kitchen and up the stairs.

I can imagine many more days and nights spent in this loft above her kitchen, exploring each other in the bed. Or eating Chinese food and watching a movie. As long as I'm with Parker, I don't care what we do.

Chapter 28

"We're not here to play it safe. We're here to glitter and win."

PARKER

"A tree trimming contest?" Jeremy asks. "But Christmas is nearly here. Shouldn't all the trees be trimmed by now?"

"Come on, Scrooge. It won't hurt you to have some fun."

"I don't know. I think I broke my funny bone when you kicked me."

I glare at him. "It wasn't my fault."

He smirks. "The sex made you do it?"

"Whatever. We're going to be late."

"We wouldn't want to be late to a tree trimming contest."

"For every minute we're late, we have to drink a shot of moonshine. Do you know how hard it is to balance on a ladder and place a mermaid ornament on a tree after several shots of moonshine?"

He growls. "You are not getting on a ladder after several shots of moonshine."

I grin. "I guess you'll be on ladder duty today."

"You're sneaky."

"Duh." I roll my eyes. "I'm a smuggler. What do you expect?"

He shakes his head. "I'm starting to understand why Eli lives on Smuggler's Hideaway."

My heart bangs in my chest. Is he falling in love with the island? Smuggler's Hideaway is famous for its ability to bewitch men. But considering the way Jeremy is staring at me, maybe I'm the one bewitching him.

My breath gets caught in my throat. What I wouldn't do to keep Jeremy on the island. I've considered kidnapping him but his hand is practically glued to his phone. I'd never get away with it. And, as we've established, I am not capable of surviving in jail.

We arrive at the little park off the main drag in Smuggler's Rest. Usually, the park has a little gazebo and a few benches. Not at Christmas time.

The area now boasts two dozen Christmas trees. Two dozen undecorated Christmas trees, which we are going to spend the next hour decorating.

"What do we get when we win this?" Jeremy asks.

"You're assuming we're going to win."

He shrugs. "You're obsessed with Christmas, and I'm an engineer. Naturally, we're going to win."

I giggle. "You're a *software* engineer."

"The principal's the same."

"Developing software is the same as building a bridge?"

He doesn't have a chance to answer before Eli flags us down. "Over here."

Jeremy strangles my hand as we walk toward the gazebo where all of the contestants are gathered.

"Are you okay?" I whisper to him.

I'm proud to be with Jeremy. Proud for everyone on the island to know he's my man. For now. At least. But maybe he doesn't want people to know. Jeremy is a very private person after all.

"I'm sorry." His grip on my hand eases.

My brow wrinkles. Why is he apologizing? Was us getting together some kind of joke? A dare? Am I the butt of the joke?

"I knew it!" Paisley squeals as she rushes toward us. "I knew you would be the perfect couple. I'm so glad I matched you."

"Matched us?"

She waves her hand in dismissal. "I sent Jeremy to you when he needed a place to stay."

"And now she thinks she's a matchmaker and we should name our first child after her," Jeremy mutters.

"I'm not picky. You can name your second child after me."

Are we seriously discussing children? Jeremy and me having children? We literally decided to try for 'more' yesterday and now we've moved on to children?

"You're crazy."

Paisley rolls her eyes. "I'm not crazy. I've been tested."

Eli strolls our way and throws an arm around her shoulders. "Ignore her. She hasn't shut up about her new matchmaking business all day."

"I'm confused. I thought you were a woman of science."

She grins. "Which means I love to experiment."

Eli slaps a hand over her mouth. "Ignore her. She's sleep deprived."

I wag my finger at her. "You're lucky you have a baby at home. Otherwise, I wouldn't be responsible for my reaction."

"I bet I could smuggle chocolate into jail for you." Jeremy winks at me.

"Don't tempt me."

"Smugglers!" Lana claps her hands to gain everyone's attention. "Smugglers! It's time to begin."

Everyone quiets down to listen to the mayor.

"For those of you who are new," her gaze settles on Jeremy. "And for those of you who prefer to cheat." She glares at Eli, who motions to Paisley and mouths, *She's the cheater.*

The mayor clears her throat. "Here are the rules. You have one hour to decorate your tree. Every fifteen minutes, you'll take a shot of *Buccaneer's Holiday Moonshine.* All decorations must come from the committee's stash. You'll be judged on theme cohesion. If our panel of judges can't guess your theme, you're out!"

Jennifer arrives with a tray of shots and begins passing them around. Once everyone has a shot glass, Lana holds up her glass. "Here's to the smugglers. Masters of the sneaky sips and secret stashes."

"Thanks for keeping the party alive!" The group responds before everyone downs their shot.

"Holy shit." Jeremy sputters and coughs.

"You okay there?"

"The cinnamon kick got me."

Eli grins. "It's our Cinnamon Sugar Cookie Moonshine. The vanilla and brown sugar are sweet, but the cinnamon gets you every time."

"And we have to drink one of these every fifteen minutes?"

"Welcome to Smuggler's Hideaway."

Jennifer bustles toward us with a clipboard. She indicates two trees next to each other in the front by the road. "Those are your trees."

I thank the town secretary before leading Jeremy to our tree.

"Why do we have to be next to the road?" he grumbles.

"Because everyone knows we're going to win."

"Ha!" Eli shouts. "We're winning."

I wag a finger at him. "No cheating this year."

"How can you possibly cheat at a tree trimming contest?" Jeremy asks.

I sigh. "Landlubbers are silly sometimes."

"You have five minutes to discuss your theme with your partner," Lana shouts. "If you put any decorations on your tree, you will be disqualified, Eli Raider."

"What if I put decorations on our tree?" Paisley asks.

"I'll tell everyone here about the time you were interviewed by the FBI for—"

"I get it!" Paisley shouts.

"Hold on. I wanted to hear about this," Eli says.

She rolls her eyes. "Liar. You were there. You know exactly what happened."

He shrugs. "Maybe I wanted the town to know."

"Good." I rub my hands together. "If they're busy bickering, they'll be distracted and won't win."

"You really want to win this thing. What's the prize?" Jeremy asks.

"The honor of knowing you're the best tree decorator on Smuggler's Hideaway. And free admission to *Barnacles & Barnyards* for two for an entire year."

"What's *Barnacles & Barnyards?*" He holds up his hand. "Never mind. Let's win this. We need a theme. I'm assuming you want to do something mermaid related."

"Nope. Everyone does mermaids or shipwrecks or smugglers. I have a better idea."

"Are you going to tell me your idea?"

I scan the area. "Nope. Too many ears. You just follow my orders and we'll be fine."

He growls. "I prefer to give the orders."

I bounce on my toes. "Not tonight, you don't."

His eyes darken. "You're going to pay for this later."

I smirk. "I hope so."

"Do not be cute and sexy. I am not climbing a ladder after three shots of moonshine with a hard-on."

"But after two shots is okay?"

He tweaks my nose. "You're trouble, Princess."

"I'm a smuggler. What did you expect?"

"I didn't expect you," he whispers as he leans close.

"You may begin now!" Lana shouts before his lips can meet mine.

"Hold that thought." I run toward the table with the approved decorations from the committee. They have exactly what I want to fit my theme. I pile Jeremy's arms full before rushing back to our tree.

"This is so much fun."

"I'm confused."

I slap Jeremy's shoulder. "Wait until my vision comes together."

Fifteen minutes later, Jennifer arrives with another round of moonshine. "Go ahead," she nods to the shot when Jeremy hesitates.

"The second shot is better." I raise my glass. "To smugglers, bootleggers, rumrunners, and the mermaids who loved them!"

"To the smugglers!" Several people shout back.

Jeremy grimaces but he downs his shot. "Is everyone on the island drunk all the time?"

"Of course not." I huff. "We don't drink and swim in the ocean. We're not stupid. Although, some people." I nod to Paisley. "Drink and ride roller coasters until they throw up on their fellow merrymakers."

"I thought Eli married a nerd."

"I'm a chemistry geek," Paisley corrects him.

I push him toward the tree. "Less talking, more decorating."

I wave to Jennifer when she arrives with the next round of shots. Jeremy groans behind me. "How many shots is this now?"

I study him. Despite how chilly it is, his face is flushed, and he's sweating.

"Do you want me to drink your shot?"

He grunts.

"It's okay. It's not against the rules. Paisley, the chemistry geek, read the rules." I lean close to whisper, "She is kind of a nerd."

"You're not drinking my shot," Jeremy grumbles before downing the moonshine.

There are only fifteen minutes left, so I skip the toast. It's crunch time.

"I think I'm finally starting to understand your theme," Jeremy says as he places our last tentacle.

"It's awesome, isn't it?"

He throws an arm over my shoulders. "If you think it's awesome, it is."

"Fifteen seconds, contestants!" Lana shouts.

I study our tree. It's perfect. This is my year. We're going to win. I glance over at Paisley and Eli's tree. I roll my eyes. They went with a classic theme. Mini liquor bottles are spread out over their tree. Guessing by the way Eli is swaying, some of those liquor bottles weren't empty but they are now.

"Five!" Lana begins the countdown and everyone joins in. "Four! Three! Two! One!"

"Come on." I lead Jeremy to the gazebo. "We'll have our last shot while the judges do their thing."

Jeremy stomps his shoes. "It's getting cold out here."

"You obviously haven't had enough moonshine."

We gather next to Eli and Paisley as we drink our shots and wait for the judges to announce the winners.

"I bet our tree wins," Eli goads Jeremy.

Jeremy shrugs. "It was my first time. I've heard it gets better after the first time."

I bark out a laugh. "Do you always revert to schoolboy humor around Eli?"

"Yes." Paisley fiddles with her glasses. "They do."

"We have a winner!" Lana shouts.

"That was quick," Jeremy says.

"If they figure out a theme super fast, that tree will win."

"Parker Shaw, come on down! Your Kraken Christmas tree is a winner."

"Hey! I helped," Jeremy complains.

Lana snorts. "This tree has Parker written all over it. Who else would fill a tree with tentacles?"

"No fair," Paisley says. "Our tree…"

Eli drags her away. "We'll see you at the *Masquerade Ball*!"

I wave to them. "How should we celebrate our win?"

"I vote for somewhere inside where it isn't snowing."

"It's snowing?" I glance up at the sky and sure enough, white flakes are falling down. "I love snow."

"I'm starting to understand the appeal," Jeremy says but he isn't gazing into the sky. He's staring at me.

My breath hitches. Does he mean me? Is he falling for me the way I'm falling for him? Dare I hope this relationship won't end in disaster? Dare I—

Nope. I cut those thoughts off. I agreed to try for more with Jeremy. I'm not going to second guess every single thought I have. I'm going to enjoy our time together.

"Me too," I whisper to him. I'm definitely not referring to the snow.

Chapter 29

"And here I thought moonshine was the most dangerous thing on this island."

JEREMY

My fingers fly over the keyboard as I work on the *Synq* app. I'm almost finished. Despite not pulling all-nighters since I've been spending most of my time with Parker, I'm nearly there.

Parker's a miracle worker. Inspiration seems to flow through me when she's near. Which is my excuse for working in the bakery while she bakes in the kitchen. Enjoying coffee breaks and lunch with her is a mere bonus. Sneaking kisses and caresses of her curvy body is the best bonus.

I don't know how I'm going to leave this island and return to California. This from a man who refused to leave California to attend college. But California no longer holds any appeal to me.

Coming to Smuggler's Hideaway for Thanksgiving was a Hail Mary but it was the best damn Hail Mary in the history of Hail Marys. This crazy, mermaid and smuggler-obsessed island has grown on me. Would it be so bad to live here permanently?

"He's here! I found him."

No. It can't be. Wherever *she* goes, my parents follow. How the hell did they find me?

I sneak a peek at the door to the kitchen. It's all the way across the bakery. I'll never make it there without her noticing.

"Jeremy! I can see you!" she shouts as she bangs on the window.

I slam my computer shut before standing and prowling to the door. No one bangs on Parker's window. I yank it open. "Do not bang on the window."

"What do you expect? You were planning to sit there and pretend you didn't hear me."

I don't deny it since she's right. If I could pretend she didn't exist now, I would.

"Mom! Dad!" She waves across the street. "I found him!"

I inhale a deep breath. I will remain calm. I will not allow my family to wind me up.

Mom and Dad hurry across the street. Mom flashes me a smile. It's about as real as her hair color.

"Darling." She leans over to kiss me but I step back before she can touch me. She frowns but doesn't remark on my unwillingness for us to touch. The first clue she doesn't give a rat's ass about me.

"Are you going to let us in?" Dad doesn't wait for an answer before shoving his way past me inside the bakery. My sister and Mom follow him.

My sister, Nora, scans the bakery and sticks her nose in the air. "This is quaint."

"If it's not good enough for you, go."

"We're not going anywhere until we've had a discussion with you," Dad says.

I scratch my neck. "How did you find me anyway?"

"It was easy. I have an alert set for whenever your face pops up on social media." Nora snorts. "And you're supposed to be some kind of computer genius."

"I'm not on social media."

"No, but this Podunk town is. Congratulations on winning the ugliest tree contest."

I swear under my breath. I didn't think twice about having my picture taken with Parker when we won the tree trimming contest the other night. I figured the town would hang the picture up in the town hall, not put it on social media.

The door to the kitchen swings open and Parker marches out. She comes to stand next to me and fists her hands on her hips. "You need to leave."

Dad bristles. "You can't kick us out."

"Wrong. I'm the proprietor of this establishment and I reserve the right to refuse service to anyone for any reason." She points to the door. "I'm invoking my right to refuse you service."

Mom bristles. "But we haven't done anything wrong."

Nora rolls her eyes. "She wants us to make a purchase. I'll have a skinny mocha latte with oat milk."

"The coffee shop is on the boulevard."

"Figures. This place is stuck in the previous century." Nora couldn't appear more bored if she tried.

"I asked you politely. Don't make me get mean."

I tug on Parker's hand. "It's okay, Princess. I'll deal with them."

"Nope. You are not dealing with these blood sucking assholes, a mermaid wouldn't be bothered to save from drowning."

"I'm confused," Mom says. "Who's drowning?"

"No one's drowning and no one's leaving," Dad insists. "I know my rights. You can't kick us out."

"You're wrong. I can kick you out."

Dad's nostrils flare. "I am not wrong. I'm calling my lawyer."

"Go ahead." She flicks her hand at him. "Spend more money you don't have proving you're wrong. You'd think you'd be tired of lawyers and judges explaining you're wrong by now."

"You don't know what you're talking about. Don't interfere where you're not wanted." Spittle flies from his mouth as he sneers at her.

I step in front of Parker. "Be nice or I'll extend the restraining order."

Parker pushes me out of her way. "I've explained this before. You don't have to protect me. It's my job to protect you from these vultures."

"Princess."

"Nope." She slams up a hand. "I don't want to hear it. I'm not allowing these people who are not your family to hurt you. Not anymore. And not on my watch."

Mine. The word reverberates through my mind. This woman is mine. I'm not letting her go. Not now. Not ever.

I love her. And this is what love is supposed to feel like. Someone who stands beside you, who fights for you, who shields you when the world turns ugly. Not someone who sees you as a walking bank account and drags you into court when you refuse to pay up.

"You should leave before I let the kraken loose," Parker tells my family and I chuckle.

"What the hell is a kraken? Does she have a guard dog? I don't want to ruin these shoes." Nora clutches her chest.

Parker barks out a laugh. "Because ruining your shoes is your biggest concern." She glances up at me. "Was she always clueless?"

"I'm not answering. I enjoy my eyeballs where they are."

"Please, as if I'd let her near you. I learned to fight on Smuggler's Hideaway. She can't get anywhere near your eyes when she's curled up on the floor crying."

I throw an arm around her shoulders. "I'm liking Smuggler's Hideaway more and more."

"Us Podunk towns tend to grow on a person."

"I'm sorry. From the depth of my heart, I can't apologize enough for saying this is a Podunk town." Especially not after my sister used the word as an insult.

"It's okay. You can make it up to me later." She waggles her eyebrows.

Dad clears his throat. "Did you forget we're standing here?"

"I didn't," Parker says. "But you apparently don't know how to listen, so now I'm ignoring you."

The bakery windows rattle with the wail of an approaching siren. A moment later, a police car slams to a stop at the curb in front of the bakery. My brow furrows as two police officers climb out of the vehicle.

Dad glares at me. "Did you call the police on us?"

"I didn't."

"I did," Cindy hollers from where she's standing behind the counter. "I don't put up with parents emotionally abusing their children in my presence."

"We are going to have a serious talk one of these days," Parker says.

"Just as soon as you explain why you're not living in the loft above the bakery, we'll have our sit-down."

Parker scowls at her before returning her attention to our group.

The bell above the door chimes as the two police officers stroll inside.

"Hi, Lucas! Hi, Weston!" Parker waves in greeting. "If you're here to find out what special Christmas pie I'm baking this year, I'm not telling."

Lucas groans. "I still haven't lost the five pounds I gained from eating your Thanksgiving pies."

"I have. You just need to find the right exercise." Weston winks.

Lucas frowns. "I have a teenager who has impeccable timing."

"How is Natalia?" Parker asks.

He grunts. "Typical teenager who knows more than I do."

My gaze dips to Parker's stomach. I can imagine it round with our child. A child she would love unconditionally because Parker doesn't know how to love any other way.

A child she would never give up on. Because Parker is loyal to her bones. She's even suffering to pay back her parents, who don't deserve her love or loyalty.

"And getting into all kinds of trouble because her mom is Chloe, the wild child?" Parker asks.

Lucas's grin is full of love. "She's a troublemaker."

"Excuse me," Dad says in a loud, entitled voice.

I grit my teeth as embarrassment fills me at his behavior. Why he thinks he's better than everyone else in the world is beyond me. The only activity he excels at is spending money he doesn't have.

Weston rests his hands on his utility belt. "Can we help you?"

"This woman." He waves a hand toward Parker and I growl. She pats my stomach to calm me down. "Is trying to kick us out of the bakery."

"Is this true, Parker?" Weston asks.

Parker narrows her eyes at my family. "They are not welcome in my bakery or on Smuggler's Hideaway."

Lucas herds my family toward the door. "Let's go. Weston and I will escort you off the island."

"Well, I never…" Mom declares.

Once my family's in the backseat, the patrol car rolls out, red and blue lights strobing, siren slicing through the air.

As soon as they're gone, Parker turns to me. "Before you say anything, I have no regrets. Yes, they're your parents but they were assholes and I won't allow anyone to treat you the way they did."

"I wasn't going to complain."

"You weren't?"

"Nope." I grasp her hand and drag her toward the kitchen. "I'm going to thank you instead."

"You are?" The question comes out all breathy.

I can't wait to take her breath away. It's too early to tell her I love her but I can show her. Which is exactly what I plan to do.

Chapter 30

"There's a first time for everything. Even for me."

JEREMY

I pause in the kitchen. "Do you have anything in the ovens that needs to come out within the next hour?"

Parker's nose wrinkles in confusion. "The ovens?"

I caress her cheek. "The ovens in the kitchen, Princess. Is the fire department going to show up because another smoke alarm went off?"

"I've got it," Holly says. "But I wouldn't mind the fire department making another appearance."

Parker grunts. "Everyone acts as if the fire department shows up on a regular basis."

"Because they do," Holly says.

"Don't exaggerate or I won't teach you how to make my Siren's Snaps cookies."

"My boyfriend loves those cookies. Consider my lips sealed." Holly mimics zipping her lips shut.

"Just to be clear. There are no imminent smoke alarms?" I ask. Holly and Parker nod. "Good. We'll see you tomorrow."

"Have fun!" Holly waves to us.

I don't need any further encouragement. It's time to show the woman I love how much I love her. Without saying the words, since it's way too early for love declarations.

I lead Parker out of the kitchen and up the stairs to the loft. As soon as we're inside, I make sure to lock the door. No one's disturbing us.

I press her against the door. "I'm going to strip you bare and taste every inch of you."

Her eyes widen and she leans toward me before shaking her head. "Are you ok?"

I thrust my hard cock against her stomach. "Does it feel as if I'm not okay?"

She clutches my biceps. "N–n–no. But the scene downstairs was messy and a bit heartbreaking."

I frame her face with my hands. "I stopped being hurt by what my parents and sister do a long time ago. They don't deserve my love or loyalty."

The same way her parents don't deserve her love or loyalty. I don't push her on the matter. My princess is stubborn. I'll show her what real love is and hopefully she'll figure out for herself how horrible her parents are.

"They don't deserve you at all," she growls.

"Thank you."

Her brow wrinkles. "Why are you thanking me?"

"For being loyal to me."

She rolls her eyes. "Of course, I'm loyal to you. You're the man I l—" She clears her throat. "You're the man I'm in a relationship with."

My heart stutters in my chest. Was she going to say the man she loves? Does she love me the way I love her? I hope so. Because I am not letting this woman go.

I meld my lips to hers and she immediately opens up for me. I allow her taste of coffee, sugar, and a hint of sea to wash over me. This is the taste of the woman I love. The taste of the woman I plan to spend my life with.

I crush her body against the door and grind my cock against her stomach. She groans and I hitch one of her legs over my hip. There. Now I can grind against her core.

She yanks my shirt out of my jeans before sneaking her hands under the material to caress my chest. I moan at the feel of her hands roaming over my body.

We have too many clothes on. I drop her leg and step back to whip my t-shirt off. Her eyes flare, and she licks her bottom lip as her gaze roams over my naked chest.

"Arms up," I order.

I grasp the hem of her shirt and yank it off her body, leaving her in a plain black bra. I don't care how her bra is plain. She doesn't need to wear lingerie for me. She's real and genuine. Exactly what I crave.

I snap her jeans open and glide my hand inside. I ignore her clit and dive straight into her pussy.

"You're wet for me."

"Duh. You're sexy and I know how good you can make me feel."

I smirk. "I make you feel good."

She rolls her eyes. "Don't gloat. It's unbecoming."

"Let's see how many times I can make you feel good and then decide whether I'm allowed to gloat."

"Such a man," she mutters.

I thrust my cock into her stomach. "Damn straight. I'm a man."

She rests her hands on my shoulders. "You gonna prove it?"

Hell, yeah, I am. I thrust my finger in and out of her a few times. I add another finger, and her walls begin to tighten. I grind my palm against her clit as I continue to tease her pussy.

"Are you going to come for me, Princess?"

"Yes," she breathes out.

"Are you going to scream my name?"

"God," she moans.

"Not god. Jeremy."

I nibble along her jaw and down her neck. She tilts her head to the side to grant me better access. She's panting now. She's close.

"Come for me, Princess. Come all over my fingers and I'll give you my cock."

I bite down on her earlobe and her pussy convulses as she climaxes.

"Jeremy," she moans.

I continue to glide my fingers in and out of her until her orgasm wanes. She collapses against me and I remember we're standing at the door.

Shit. This is not the way to show Parker I love her.

I lift her into my arms and carry her to the bed, where I gently lay her down. Her eyes flutter open.

"What are you doing?"

I smirk. "Moving onto phase two."

She smiles and it hits me directly in the heart. I want to watch her smile up at me in bed for the rest of my life. This woman owns my heart and I have gladly handed it over to her.

"Someone needs to be naked in order for me to make her feel good."

She giggles. "I'm pretty sure you can make me feel good while I'm still dressed."

"True, but I want to feel your naked body against mine while I slide into you."

Her breath hitches. "I agree to this plan."

I chuckle. "Glad I have your agreement."

I quickly undress her before chucking off my jeans. She widens her legs and I climb onto the bed.

"I thought for sure you'd steal a pair of handcuffs from Weston or Lucas."

"Next time. I want you to be able to touch me today." I want to feel the hands of the woman I love caress me as I make love to her.

"Good. I love touching you."

I claim her lips. She wraps her arms and legs around me as I explore her mouth. I'm a lucky bastard. I get to taste and explore this mouth for the rest of my life.

If Parker thinks she can get rid of me, she has another thing coming. I am not letting her go.

She rubs her breasts against my chest and I moan at the feel of her hard nipples against my skin. I love her breasts. I could play with them all morning.

I tear my mouth from hers to nibble my way down to those magnificent mounds of flesh I'm obsessed with. I latch onto a nipple and her hands thread through my hair to push me down. Don't worry, Parker. I'm not going anywhere.

I tease her nipple until she's grinding against me. Her wet heat is only inches from my hard cock. With a small movement, I could slide into her.

But I hold back. I want to tease her until she's begging me.

"One of these days, I'm going to fuck these breasts."

She squirms beneath me. She likes the idea. Good to know.

I release her nipple with a pop and get to my knees. I notch my cock at her entrance. I inch inside. Damn, she feels good. Better than anything I've experienced before.

I glance down to watch my cock enter her pussy and swear.

"What's wrong?"

"I forgot a condom."

I never forget protection. Being a billionaire means women would do anything to bear my child. I've caught more than one woman poking holes in a condom. Which is why I always bring my own.

"Um…" Parker nibbles on her bottom lip.

I remove her lip from her teeth with my teeth before sweeping my tongue over the area. "What?"

"We don't need a condom."

I freeze. I've never had sex without a condom. Not even in my drunken college days before I developed my first app was I reckless enough to forget protection.

I growl. "What did you say?"

"Forget it. I'll grab a condom."

She reaches for the drawer but I shackle her wrist to stop her.

"You're serious?"

She shrugs. "I'm on birth control."

She's not lying. I've seen the pills on the vanity in the bathroom.

"And you trust me?"

I hold my breath as I wait for her to answer. I want her to trust me.

She rolls her eyes. "Of course, I trust you. I wouldn't be here in this bed with you if I didn't trust you."

Warmth fills me. She trusts me. It's not love, but it's a start. I'll convince her to fall in love with me. Starting now.

"Thank you, Princess. And, in case there's any doubt, I trust you. I've never had sex without a condom. I've never even considered it. But I want to slide into you bare. I want to feel you without anything between us."

She widens her legs. "Let's make this happen."

I laugh but when I notch my cock at her entrance again, the laughter dries up to be replaced with passion and possession.

Parker is mine. No one else will touch her.

I inch inside until my balls slap against her ass. "You feel good," I grit out.

"You too," she breathes out.

Good is an understatement. She feels fucking fantastic. I just found my favorite place to be. Buried deep inside the woman I love.

And now it's time to show her how much I love her.

Chapter 31

"Christmas is coming. So is reality."

PARKER

I snuggle into Jeremy's warmth. I don't feel the need to run away. This is where I belong. With Jeremy.

I don't want to let him go. Especially after the scene with his parents. He needs to experience how love and loyalty feels because his parents didn't give him that kind of love. They didn't give him love at all.

My brow wrinkles. I'm using the word love an awful lot today.

Because you love Jeremy.

I don't…. I stop the thought before the lie is fully formed. I'm done lying to myself. I love Jeremy, plain and simple. I was powerless to stop myself from falling for him.

Because Jeremy is perfect. He's sweet and funny and makes my toes curl with a single kiss.

He also listens to me – really listens to me. He doesn't try to bulldoze me. Unlike my parents, who become deaf whenever I open my mouth. They don't even try to understand me.

I want to wake up every morning in Jeremy's arms. But I can't. My stomach sours. Jeremy isn't here to stay.

Sure, he said we should try for 'more,' but everyone knows long-distance relationships don't work. I've seen the movies and read the books. I know how it goes.

At first, you're into each other and visit each other as often as possible. Soon enough, life gets in the way and you can't manage to visit as often. Before you know it, you're heartbroken, lying on the floor in the bakery, cuddling Viking while eating a chocolate cake.

Jeremy's phone rings and he groans before rolling over to answer it.

"What?" he barks into the phone.

I start to get out of bed but he captures my hand to stop me. "Where are you going?"

I yank my hand from his. "To give you some privacy."

"Hold on, Chuck." He mutes the phone. "Why do you need to give me privacy?"

I roll my eyes. "Because you run a billion-dollar business." He grunts. "Maybe I'm a corporate spy and I got into your pants to steal all your ideas for apps."

He barks out a laugh and I glare at him.

"Sorry." He clears his throat. "You're a corporate spy?"

"I could be a spy."

"You bake too well to be a spy. Besides, you can't lie for shit."

"I can, too!"

He nods to my hand where I'm scratching my palm. "Damn the pirates. You couldn't pretend to not notice?"

"Why would I pretend to not notice? Noticing you and all the crazy shit you do is the highlight of my life."

"I don't do crazy shit."

He lifts a brow. "And you don't have an otter for a pet either."

I stick out my bottom lip. "Viking's living at the restaurant since someone…" I glare at him, "is afraid of him."

He sighs. "Fine. Bring Viking over here."

"And you'll cuddle him?"

"Don't push your luck, Princess."

"Can I go use the bathroom now while you answer your call?"

"Go. I enjoy watching your ass when you walk away." He returns to his phone call and I make sure to sway my ass as I walk to the bathroom.

I take my time getting ready since Jeremy's on the phone. No matter what he says, he deserves privacy to deal with business.

When I finally emerge from the bathroom, Jeremy is still on the phone.

"Fine. I'll be there." He hangs up and throws the phone onto the bed. "Damnit."

"What's wrong?" I hold up my hand before he can answer. "I'm sorry. I shouldn't have asked. It's none of my business."

He stalks toward me. Unfortunately, he put on his sweat-pants while he was on the phone. But his chest is still on display, so I still get to ogle him while he approaches.

"Eyes up here, Princess."

"But I had a pretty view."

"My face isn't a pretty view?"

"Maybe if you smile and your dimples are on display."

He smiles and I watch his dimples appear. Yep, it's a pretty view, too.

"Now." He grasps my hands and yanks. I fly forward into his body. His hard body I enjoy touching.

I lift my hands but he shackles my wrists. "Serious discussion time."

"Uh oh. Am I in trouble? Are you going to spank me?" I joke since 'discussion time' doesn't bode well for me. Maybe Jeremy has decided a long-distance relationship is too difficult. Is he done with me already?

"Don't distract me, Princess."

I raise an eyebrow. "Was it working?"

He studies me. "Maybe it would work if you were naked."

"I can be naked in two seconds flat."

"As much as I'd enjoy watching you fail, we do need to have a serious discussion."

"What?" I pout.

"We're in a relationship."

"Phew." I run the back of my hand over my forehead. "I didn't have sex with some man I don't know."

"Knock it off," he says but his lips tip up. "What I'm trying to say is that we're in a relationship and my business is your business. I don't mind you listening in on phone calls. Or knowing what's going on at *Apparoo.* I trust you."

"I trust you, too, but …"

He places a finger over my lips. "No buts. I don't want to hide or keep secrets from you."

"For not doing serious relationships, you sure know how to act in one. Is this how it's going to be? You always besting me in everything?"

"Pretty sure you can bake circles around me."

I giggle. "I can't disagree."

"Now, about business."

I clear my throat and straighten my back. "Okay, Mr. CEO. Hit me with it."

"Unfortunately, that was Chuck on the phone. He's the operations manager for *Apparoo.* There are some issues with the rollout of our new product and I need to troubleshoot."

"Does this mean you're going to California?"

And so it begins. How long will this long-distance relationship last? I won't be taking any bets on it lasting, no matter how much I love Jeremy. If he doesn't feel the same, there's no chance for us.

You don't know he doesn't feel the same.

Yes, I do. Jeremy's a straight shooter. He would have told me otherwise. But he hasn't.

He caresses my cheek. "Why don't you come with me? My penthouse has a view of the Pacific Ocean."

"I can't. It's nearly Christmas or did you forget, Scrooge?"

"I'm not Scrooge."

He isn't Scrooge anymore but it's fun to tease him.

"I have a ton of Christmas pies and cakes to bake."

"What about Holly? You've been teaching her to bake."

I snort. "Teaching. Holly is not ready to handle the Christmas rush on her own."

"Damnit. I can't delay this trip until after the holidays. The launch is in January."

"Will you be back before Christmas?"

Christmas is less than a week away. I don't want to experience Christmas without him. I want to show him all the things to love about the day. Exchanging presents, kissing under the mistletoe, dressing up as a pirate for the *Smuggler's Hideaway Masquerade Dance.*

"I will. No matter what happens, I'll be back."

"Good. Because I already reserved your pirate outfit for the dance on Christmas Eve."

He blinks. "Pirate outfit?"

"It's a masquerade dance. You have to wear a costume."

"I'll be back. I promise."

"Don't make promises you can't keep."

"Worst case scenario, I fly back for Christmas and return to California the day after."

Disappointment hits me. The week after Christmas is the slowest time of the year for the bakery. There are no special orders since everyone is usually still suffering from their gluttony over the holidays.

I was eagerly anticipating spending the time with Jeremy. This long-distance relationship stuff sucks. No wonder they don't work.

"Hey." Jeremy pinches my chin. "We're going to make this work. I'm going to do everything in my power to make sure of it."

I blow out a breath. "Okay."

There's no sense worrying about the future when I don't know what the future holds. I'm going to enjoy spending time with the man I love for as long as I can.

"When do you leave?"

He smirks. "The jet won't leave without me. Which means we have time."

"Time for what?"

"Me to show you all the reasons I plan to hurry back to Smuggler's Hideaway."

I tap my chin. "I'm intrigued. Tell me more."

His smile stretches from ear to ear and shows off his dimples. "I have to show you."

"If you must."

"Oh, I must."

He carries me to the bed and drops me on it. "You wasted time getting dressed. But now I get to enjoy stripping you."

"Go ahead and do your worst, Scrooge."

He playfully growls at the word Scrooge before getting to work on stripping me.

Maybe this long-distance relationship will work after all. Maybe I should stop worrying about the future. And maybe I should…

The thoughts fly out of my mind when Jeremy bites my inner thigh. I moan and concentrate on the moment.

Chapter 32

"Some things are worth the upheaval."

JEREMY

"Are you certain this is what you want to do?" Chuck asks.

Am I certain I want to move across the country to live with the woman I love? There's no doubt in my mind. I knew the second I stepped onto the jet to leave Smuggler's Hideaway, it was the last time I'd leave Parker behind.

"This is going to cause a lot of upheaval in the company," Jennifer, the human resources manager for *Apparoo*, adds.

The other members of the board – including Eli – haven't questioned me once since I announced my desire to move the company to the island of Smuggler's Hideaway. In fact, Eli smirked and muttered something along the lines of 'about damn time'.

"You've never done something this impulsive before," Chuck claims.

Eli barks out a laugh. "Never done something this impulsive before? Did you miss the time he thought up and developed an app while he was supposed to be on vacation? By the time he returned to the office, he had a marketing plan ready."

Chuck waves a dismissive hand in the air. "I meant impulsive as in the business. Not the apps he designs."

The apps are the business. He's the operations manager, he knows this.

"Is this because of a woman?"

I glare at him. "None of your business." Chuck is a member of the board, but we're not friends. We're colleagues.

"It is my business when a little baker from a small town in the middle of nowhere wraps you around her finger and doesn't let you come home."

Little baker from a small town? How does he know about Parker? I certainly haven't told him. Has he been spying on me? Another reason to avoid social media.

"What are you talking about?"

He rolls his eyes. "Don't avoid the question. Are we moving the entire headquarters of *Apparoo* to the middle of nowhere because a woman is leading you around by your dick?"

How dare he! Who the hell does he think he is? I jump from my chair and prowl toward him.

Eli steps in my way. "He's not worth it."

I raise an eyebrow. "What if he said those things about Paisley?"

"I'd laugh at him because he's jealous and has a small dick."

"Fine," I mutter and return to my seat. I'll let this go. I'll be the bigger man.

"Remember what happened the last time you decided a woman was 'the one'?" Chuck asks.

I growl at him. He's a liar. Before Parker, I never thought a woman was 'the one'. Hell, before Parker, I didn't have relationships that lasted more than a weekend. She's the exception to every single one of my rules.

"You ended up having to settle out of court when she threatened to sell company secrets to the highest bidder."

"I didn't tell her any secrets and you know it."

The woman in question planted a bug in my phone. She came and sat by me in a hotel bar. We had one drink together and then said our goodbyes. She tried to get me to accompany her upstairs to her hotel room, but I declined.

Parker would never do any of those things. She's too honest and loyal.

"I don't like this," Chuck continues to complain.

"And I don't like how you lied to get me to come to California when you didn't need me." I could be in Smuggler's Hideaway now with Parker. Instead, I'm in the office arguing with this asshat.

"You shouldn't be away from headquarters for a month."

Someone has gotten too big for his britches. He doesn't get to decide when or how long I'm in the office. I'm in charge here. This is my company. Being a member of the board doesn't give him license to control me.

"Who else agrees with him?" I scan the faces of the other board members. Chuck and Jennifer are the only ones nodding.

"There's a simple solution here. Anyone who doesn't want to relocate to Smuggler's Hideaway can remain in California." Chuck begins to smile. "You'll receive a generous compensation package."

Chuck scowls. "You're firing us for not wanting to relocate?"

"You can't do this," Jennifer claims.

"I can and you know it."

I didn't trust Jennifer with the news about the relocation – she's good at her job but she also enjoys gossiping in the break room entirely too much – so I hired an outside firm to handle the legalities of relocating the hundred employees at *Apparoo* headquarters to Smuggler's Hideaway.

I phoned the firm while on my way to California. Nothing is delaying this move.

I fling a file across the table toward Chuck. "The details of your severance package."

I had the package prepared in the hopes he wouldn't want to move. Chuck has never been my favorite person but when he claimed he had an emergency and forced me to fly across the country at a moment's notice for nothing, I was done.

Anyone who gets between me and Parker will find themselves on my bad side. She's my priority. Everyone else is in the backseat. If they're even in the car at all.

"Relocating is a good move for the company," Eli says. He's had my back since I made the announcement an hour ago, despite my not warning him in advance.

"You would say that," Chuck sneers. "You live on the tiny island."

"Which is why I know the operating costs will be significantly lower and there will be less competition for talent. I already have a meeting set up with the mayor to discuss tax incentives."

When did Eli manage to set up a meeting with Lana?

"The quality of life is higher as well. No traffic, no smog," I add. "Plus, this gives us a chance to shape a healthier, less toxic company culture." I meet Jennifer's gaze. "I'd think you'd be happy about these changes."

She sighs. "My kids are in high school. I can't afford to give up in-state tuition rates."

"I'm sorry to hear that." I pass her a package. "You'll find the severance pay is more than reasonable."

She flips open the folder and her eyes widen. "This is acceptable."

I made sure it would be. I'm not messing around. I own the majority shares in *Apparoo* and Eli has a significant amount of shares as well. Together, we could push this relocation through without the support of the rest of the board, but I have no desire to get caught up in litigation or delays.

I will not be away from Parker any longer than necessary. She's worried enough about us being in a long-distance relationship. She has enough worries in her life. I will not be one of them. My job is to alleviate her worries. Not add to them.

"Anyone else have any objections?"

When no one responds, I nod. "This meeting is adjourned."

Eli and I slip out of the boardroom before Chuck can corner us.

"The jet is fueled and ready to go. Are you ready?" Eli asks.

"Hell, yeah. I've been gone too long as it is." It's only been a few days but it's been a few days too many.

He claps me on the back. "Happy for you. Parker is a good woman."

"I love her."

He chuckles. "I assumed as much since you're spending several million dollars relocating the business to the island."

"With the lower operating costs and tax incentives, we'll earn the money back in less than two years."

I've done the calculations since Parker is going to lose her mind when she finds out about the move. Yes, I'm doing this for her.

But I know how guilty she gets about money. I don't want her to feel any guilt when it comes to me. It's bad enough she feels guilty about her parents paying for her to attend culinary school.

I check my watch. "Let's head directly to the airport. If we don't have too much traffic, I should make my meeting with the realtor."

"Buying a house already? When you do something, you go all in."

"This is not news to you."

He groans. "As long as you don't go all in on a keto diet again. The smell in our dorm room from your 'intestinal issues' was rank."

I shrug. "You never should have bet me I couldn't lose ten pounds in a month."

"You're as bad as my brothers."

We arrive at the airport in less than thirty minutes. Not quite a record, but fast enough to ensure I'll make my meeting with the realtor.

I dig out the house listings Jade sent me as we taxi onto the runway.

"Find anything interesting?"

"It's tough. I want to be near the bakery. Parker prefers to walk to work."

He grins. "Moving her in with you immediately?"

"I would if I could, but she's stubborn."

"All good women are."

"I'm not moving once I settle on the island. I'm ready to buy my forever home." Not an apartment. A home. I haven't had one in years and I can't wait.

Eli flips through the listings. "If she's willing to bike to work, this place isn't too far and it has an excellent view of the ocean. There's a beach as well, although all beaches on the island are public."

I study the picture of the house he indicated. It's a Cape Cod with a wraparound porch. I imagine sitting on the porch with Parker, sipping on a beer at the end of the day, while watching our children run around the front lawn.

"If it doesn't need too much work, I'll buy it."

"You haven't seen it yet."

I shrug. "I'll fix anything Parker doesn't like about it."

He smiles. "I freaking love you being in love."

"It scares the hell out of me," I admit. What if Parker doesn't love me back? What if I lose her? What if something happens to her?

He claps a hand on my shoulder in squeezes. "You're on the right track if you're scared."

"I guess I'm on the right track then."

The flight attendant appears and we order some whiskey to celebrate. I've missed my best friend. Soon, I'll be living near him and the woman I love.

I never expected when I fled to Smuggler's Hideaway to deal with my coding block, I'd end up falling in love but I wouldn't have it any other way.

Chapter 33

"Optimism may have been a bad ingredient choice."

PARKER

I sing as I prepare the dough for my Snow-drift Sirens cookies. The shortbread dipped in white chocolate with sea salt flakes is always a hit at Christmas on Smuggler's Hideaway.

On the first day of baking, my oven gave to me:

One burnt bottom crust and some sass from Viking's stare.

On the second day of baking, the smugglers begged from me:

Two rum pecan pies

And one burnt bottom crust and some sass from Viking's stare...

Viking chirps when he hears his name and I smile down at him. He's currently mad at me since he's stuck in his crate.

I wag my finger at him. "You shouldn't have jumped into the bowl with the dough for my sugar cookies. The dough was supposed to be for my North Pole Narwhal Nibbles."

He chirps again and gives me his puppy dog eyes.

I snort. "You can't fool me, Viking. I've fallen for those puppy dog eyes one too many times. I have way too much baking to do today to be distracted by you. No matter how adorable you are."

It's crunch time for the bakery. Christmas is only a few days away, and the cookies and pies are flying off the shelves.

I don't mind all the extra work. Being exhausted means I don't have the emotional bandwidth to miss Jeremy.

I'm lying. Of course, I miss Jeremy. I miss his warm body cocooning me in warmth and safety all night. I miss him trailing off mid-sentence because he thought of some brilliant idea. I miss how good he can make me feel.

I plain miss him. I miss the man who makes me feel as if I matter. Who listens to me. I'm a goner for the billionaire. No one is more surprised than me.

My phone beeps with a message. Speaking of Scrooge.

Good news. I should be home tonight.

My stomach warms. *Home.* Does he consider Smuggler's Hideaway home?

Can't wait to see you.

I'll be there soon, Princess.

I heart the message before putting my phone away and returning to work. I didn't know what to expect when Jeremy left. Would he call? Would he message? Would he go silent? I didn't dare ask.

To my delight, he didn't go silent. He calls every evening. And he messages me good morning every day.

Holly peeks her head in from the bakery. "Sorry to bother you but we have a situation out front."

"What kind of situation?"

Her nose wrinkles. "One you have to deal with."

I blow out a breath. "Fine. Give me a second to check my timers."

"No hurry," she says before disappearing.

My brow wrinkles. No hurry? What kind of situation is this?

I scan the ovens and my timers. I have ten minutes before the next batch of cookies is done. I wash my hands before making my way into the bakery.

I stop dead in my tracks when I realize what the situation is. Triton's trident. I do not want to interact with *them.*

Unfortunately, they spot me before I can sneak back into the kitchen. They smile and wave as they make their way toward me.

A small kernel of hope blossoms inside me. Maybe they're here to invite me to Christmas dinner at their house. It is the season of miracles after all.

"Hi, Mom. Dad," I greet.

"Darling." Mom kisses my cheek.

The small kernel of hope grows at the kiss. Eek! Maybe they're here to bury the hatchet. Best. Christmas. Present. Ever.

"We have something to discuss with you," Dad says.

At his calm manner, the hope inside me practically explodes. This is it. The moment I've been waiting for. My parents are going to apologize for their behavior and say how proud of me they are.

And they should be proud. The bakery is packed with customers. The line snakes through the tables of people drinking coffee and out the door.

Pirate's Pastries initially suffered when the café on the boulevard opened – especially since I didn't have the money to do extra marketing or stunts – but we've bounced back now. I won the gingerbread contest and participating in the Mermaid Treasure Hunt has brought in tons of new customers.

"Shall we sit?" I motion to the only available table in the corner of the café. The table is reserved for Jeremy but I swipe the reserved sign before my parents notice.

"Do you want a coffee?" I ask as they settle in their seats. "There's no need to wait. I can make you one."

At their nods, I hurry to the counter.

"What's going on?" Holly asks.

"I don't know, but I think it's going to be good."

She frowns. "You shouldn't get your hopes up."

"Too late," I sing as I finish the coffee for my parents.

"Here you go," I set their drinks on the table before sitting across from them. "What do you want to discuss?"

I probably appear deranged with how big my smile is but I don't care. This is the nicest my parents have been since I told them I was buying this bakery and staying in Smuggler's Hideaway.

Dad nods to Mom, who opens her purse and pulls out a slip of paper.

"We wanted you to see this before everyone on the island was talking about it behind your back."

"Behind my back?" My brow wrinkles. "What do you mean?"

Mom slides the paper across the table. There's a gleam in her eye. My stomach drops. What is happening here?

"Read it and you'll understand."

I glance at Dad but he won't meet my gaze. My fingers tremble as I pick up the newspaper clipping.

Jeremy Holland on the town with supermodel

The headline is accompanied by a photograph of Jeremy with a skinny blonde woman clinging to him.

I shake the clipping at my parents. "This is why you came here today?"

"Yes, darling." Mom's grin is calculating. Has she always been this cruel?

"We didn't want you to get your hopes up that your boyfriend would solve all your problems," Dad adds.

"Solve my problems?"

"Yes." He motions to the bakery.

"Are you clueless?" He opens his mouth to respond but I hold up my hand. "It was a rhetorical question since anyone who isn't clueless can tell the bakery is doing well. The line is out the door."

He squirms in his seat. "Yes, well."

"And I don't need a boyfriend to solve my problems. I'm a grown ass woman. I can solve my own problems."

Mom purses her lips. "And yet you didn't get an internship after finishing culinary school despite graduating at the top of your class."

"For mermaid's sake!" I explode. "You want to know why I didn't get an internship? I'll tell you. Because some asshole son of a billionaire stole my place."

Dad scowls. "Why didn't you tell us? We would have litigated."

"This is exactly why I didn't tell you. I had no interest in drawing out the entire mess with a lawsuit. I let karma do its work."

Mom rolls her eyes. "Litigation is more successful than karma."

I study her and suddenly something clicks in my mind. A thought I've been burying deep inside for a very long time. "You're never going to approve of me, are you? I could pay back all the money you spent on culinary school for me and you still wouldn't love me."

"We love you. You're our daughter," Dad claims.

"You have a funny way of showing it." I tap the newspaper clipping.

"He's cheating on you. We wanted you to know."

"Bullshit. Do you think I'm stupid? This photograph isn't recent. Jeremy's hair is much longer than it is now, and this supermodel fell from grace years ago when she was arrested for driving under the influence."

Dad suddenly finds the floor fascinating while Mom becomes obsessed with her nails. Their actions scream guilty.

"I'm such an idiot. I thought you came here to invite me to Christmas dinner."

"We're having dinner at the resort. The reservation is for two."

"I figured as much," I mutter.

"But I did speak to Hudson, he still hasn't found a pastry chef," Dad says.

I should have known. My parents and their obsession with prestige strikes again. I stand. "Goodbye."

"This is the thanks we get for raising you," Mom mutters.

Raising me? I spent my childhood with nannies and babysitters. Mom and Dad were always busy building their orthodontic practice. I thought they were hard workers. But now I realize they just couldn't be bothered with me.

I don't say a word as I make my way through the bakery to the kitchen. My timer goes off and I get to work. Except my hands shake. I drop the cookie tray on the prep table.

I can't believe I ever thought I could earn their approval or their love. I'm done trying.

Holly bustles in from the café. "Let me finish the baking."

"You're needed out front."

"I closed the café an hour early. The customers helped me clean up."

"They did?"

"After they ran your parents out."

My parents. My bottom lip trembles, and my eyes swell with unshed tears. I thought they were merely disappointed in me before. Disappointed would be better than the cruelty they've shown me today.

Holly releases Viking from his cage and hands him to me. "Go upstairs to the loft. I've got this handled."

I try to thank her but I'm afraid if I speak, the tears I'm holding back will burst out. I nod instead.

I cuddle Viking as I walk upstairs to the loft. I manage to make it inside before the first tear falls.

Chapter 34

"You're going to want to see the kitchen."

JEREMY

"You have a deal." I shake hands with Jade.

"I can't believe you chose a house this quick."

I shrug. "When I know what I want, I go after it."

The same way I went after Parker when I realized she's the one I want. It took me a while to let go of my prejudices about women. But she showed me not all women are after my money.

I can't wait to show her this house. It's perfect for a family. And it's a short bike ride from the bakery.

"Did you want to view those business listings I sent you now?"

"No need. I decided to buy the large lot of land near the distillery."

"You're going to build?"

"It's the only way to ensure I get exactly what I want." *Apparoo* has very specific requirements – climate-controlled rooms, plenty of electrical outlets with surge protection, security with biometrics, to name a few – that I won't find in an abandoned warehouse or former garage.

"Understood. I'll draw up the paperwork for both transactions."

"Thanks, Jade."

I wait until she locks up the house and then walk her to her car.

With all my business wrapped up, I settle in my new car – I can't be bothered to have my car shipped across the country – and make my way to the bakery.

The windows of *Pirate's Pastries* are dark, and it's all closed up for the day. Parker said she usually stays open longer during the holiday season. Maybe she sold out early. Good for her.

As I climb the stairs to the loft, anticipation and excitement fill me. It's only been a few days since I saw Parker but I missed her. I missed her more than I expected I would.

I plan to spend as few nights away from her as possible from now on. It'll be difficult the first year as *Apparoo* transitions to Smuggler's Hideaway, but I don't mind working hard for what I want. And Parker is what I want.

"Parker," I holler as I knock on the door. When she doesn't answer, I frown. She said she'd be home tonight waiting for me.

Waiting for me. Maybe she has a fun surprise planned. A surprise including sexy lingerie and a big bed. My cock twitches. I dig my keys out and unlock the door.

Parker is slumped on the floor. Fear ricochets through my body as I rush to her.

"What's wrong, Princess? Are you injured? Do you need the hospital?"

She lifts her head to meet my gaze and my heart stops at her tear-stained face. I don't hesitate. I gather her into my arms and settle on the bed with her.

"What happened, Princess?" I brush the hair off her face.

"M-m-my parents."

I grind my teeth. "What did they do now?"

"They showed me a newspaper clipping. It was a picture of you with another woman."

Fuck. I cup her face. "I promise I haven't been with another woman since we met. I'm not a cheater."

"I know."

Relief fills me. She believes me. She didn't question who the woman was or what happened. She believes me. End of question. Damn, I love this woman.

"Then, why all the tears?"

"My parents showed me the clipping to deliberately hurt me. They will never love me. They're never going to invite me to enjoy the holidays with them. It doesn't matter if I pay them back or not. It won't change anything."

Her parents are assholes. Who hurts their child this way?

"You don't need them. We'll build our own family."

She blinks. "Our own family?"

"I love you, and I want to build a family with you."

"You love me?"

"Why do you think I bought a house on the island and am moving the headquarters of *Apparoo* to Smuggler's Hideaway?"

Her mouth gapes open. "What?"

"It's a good investment."

"It's a good investment?"

"Yes. Between the lower operating costs and tax incentives, the company will earn the money back from the move in less than two years."

Her brow wrinkles. "Why are you telling me this?"

"Because I don't want you to feel guilty that I moved my entire company across the country to be with you."

"Y-y-ou did what?"

I caress her cheek. "I love you. I'm not living apart from you."

"You love me?"

I smile. "Yes."

"Phew. I thought the love train was one-sided."

"Love train?"

She giggles. "I love you, too."

Heat radiates through my chest. She loves me. Parker Shaw loves me. I don't enjoy the sound of her name. Parker Holland sounds better. I'll make it happen.

I meld my lips to hers. She tastes of salt from her tears and I release her with a growl.

"I don't want you to ever cry over your parents again."

She rolls her eyes. "You can't order me not to cry over my parents."

"Yes, I can. I just did."

"I'm not one of your employees." She clears her throat. "Are you seriously moving your company to Smuggler's Hideaway?"

"Yep. I bought the land today."

"You bought the land already? You're pretty sure of yourself."

"I told you I am not living apart from you. I figured I'd need some time to get you to fall in love with me but you already love me, so we're good."

"We're good?"

"Yep. How many children do you want?"

"Whoa. You need to slow down."

"Okay." I nod. "I'll slow down." Not much, but I can pretend. "We won't move into our new house together immediately."

"Our new house?"

"I bought it today. Do you want to see pictures?" I dig out my phone. "It's a Cape Cod with a wraparound porch."

She gasps at the picture. "I love this house."

"You know it?"

"Yeah. I used to bike past it on my way to school every morning. An elderly couple lived there and they'd be sitting on the porch drinking their coffee. If I recall, they died recently but none of their children wanted the house. They all moved away from the island."

"Have you ever been inside?" She shakes her head. "You're going to love it. The first floor is all open concept. Wherever you are, you can look out of the big windows and view the ocean. The kitchen needs renovating. You're in charge there. I want you to have everything you need to bake cookies with our children on Saturday mornings."

"So much for slowing down on the kids thing," she mutters.

I grin. "You need to know what the kitchen will be used for before you design it."

"You're crazy."

"Crazy in love with you."

She giggles. "Who knew Scrooge could fall in love?"

"And without those scary ghosts visiting me, too."

She wags her finger. "It's not Christmas Eve yet. Maybe they'll still come."

I groan. "You're going to dress up as a ghost and scare me, aren't you?"

"Not now since you figured out my plan."

I dive for her ribs. She bats my hands away. "I'm not ticklish."

"Maybe I haven't found your ticklish spot yet. I'm willing to put in the work to find it." I waggle my eyebrows.

Her breath hitches. "We're really doing this?"

"Planning a life together? Hell, yeah, we are."

"But we've only known each other a month."

"Don't care. When I know what I want, I go for it."

"And you want me?"

I kiss her hair. "I love you, Princess. I want to spend my life with you. I want to spend every night wrapped around you. Spend every morning drinking coffee with you. I can't wait until you agree to move into our house. Although, I need to add extra smoke alarms first."

She slaps at my chest. "I don't cause fires all the time!"

"And I don't have the Smuggler's Hideaway Fire Department on speed dial."

She narrows her eyes at me. "Now, you've done it."

She dives for my ribs. Unlike her, I am ticklish. I manage to shackle her hands and roll her over until I'm looming above her. Her chest heaves as she stares up at me. Her love for me is clear to see in her blue eyes. Blue eyes, I hope our children inherit.

"I love you, Princess. I can't wait to start our life together."

She wraps her legs around my waist and rubs herself against my cock. "Why wait?"

"Fair warning. I will use sex to convince you to move in with me and have my babies."

She smirks. "You can try."

I plan to try over and over again. Until I've wrung every orgasm possible out of her body. Until we're both sated. For the moment. I will never be completely sated when it comes to Parker.

"I love you," I whisper before I press my lips to hers.

Chapter 35

"Don't be a party pooper, Scrooge. It's Christmas time."

PARKER

"Wake up! Wake up!" I bounce on the bed to wake Jeremy.

He groans. "What time is it?"

"It's Christmas time!"

He shakes his head. "It's Christmas Eve. Not Christmas yet."

"Don't be mean, mister or I'll sic Viking on you."

Viking chirps in agreement from where he's nestled on a pillow in front of the heater with the lights from the Christmas tree illuminating him. I smile at him. I couldn't be happier to have him with me. He's not going anywhere since I no longer have to worry about paying my parents back.

After the stunt they played in my bakery, I'm done. Until they apologize, they are not part of my life.

I've already given my notice at my apartment. Jeremy couldn't be happier. Naturally. He got what he wanted. Which was what I wanted as well but still. He doesn't need to gloat.

Jeremy sighs before sitting up in bed and propping the pillows up behind him. "Why are you up this early? The bakery is closed today and tomorrow."

Since Jeremy finished his app two days ago, he was able to help me in the bakery. Together, we managed to finish all the Christmas orders and get them delivered yesterday. And now we have two glorious days off together to enjoy the holiday.

I hand him a cup of cocoa. "It's time to open presents."

I came home yesterday to discover a mountain of presents under my little Christmas tree. It's a good thing I'm not a cat or I would have expired from curiosity. My first Christmas presents from Jeremy.

"Christmas presents shouldn't be opened until Christmas Day."

"Don't be a party pooper, Scrooge. Let's start a new tradition. We each open one present on Christmas Eve morning."

His eyes widen when he notices the two presents I already chose are waiting on the corner of the bed.

He sips from his cocoa while he stares at me over the rim of the mug. I bat my eyelashes in a silent plea. Finally, he sets the cocoa down on the nightstand. "Okay."

I squeal and dive for the presents.

"But I get to pick the present you open."

I frown.

"I pick the present or you wait to open all your presents until tomorrow."

"Fine."

He chuckles at my pout before crawling out of bed. He chooses the largest box under the tree and hands it to me.

I bounce on the bed. "Oh. I wonder what it is." I shake the box. I can feel rattling inside. "It's light. But the box is big."

He settles behind me and wraps his arms around me. "Open it and find out."

I tear into the wrapping paper and he chuckles. "You don't save the paper?"

"Shush you." I open the box only to discover there's another box inside. "How many boxes are there? Am I unwrapping a present or a Russian doll family Christmas?"

He rests his chin on my shoulder. "You'll see."

I remove the box. It's also covered in wrapping paper. I quickly get rid of it before opening it to discover another box. I growl. "How many boxes are there?"

"I figured I'd need several or you'd manage to unwrap it and discover what's inside before Christmas."

I gasp. "Are you saying I snoop?"

"I'm saying I caught you unwrapping one of the presents under the tree."

I sniff and stick my nose in the air. "I don't know what you're talking about."

"Sure, you don't." He points to the box. "You gonna open it?"

"If there isn't a present at the end of this torture, I'm not going to let you open your presents until Valentine's Day."

"Don't care. I have everything I want in my arms now."

I melt into him. "You say the nicest things."

He kisses my neck. "Open the present."

There are two more empty boxes before I reach an envelope. "If this is a check or money, you are seriously going to experience the Christmas ghosts and they are going to terrify you."

"It's not money or a check."

I narrow my eyes at him. He doesn't scratch his neck. Huh. He appears to be truthful. I guess we'll see. I open the envelope and read the card. My jaw drops open.

"Are you serious?" He nods. "We're going to Paris?"

"I want to show you all the wonderful patisseries and the Eiffel Tower. We'll dine outside in Montmartre. We'll visit the Louvre to see the Mona Lisa. And—"

"We're going to Paris!" I scream.

I tackle him and rain kisses over his face. "Thank you. Thank you. Thank you. When do we go? I need to figure out the bakery. Is my passport still valid?"

I try to jump from the bed to go check but he snatches my wrist to stop me. "We can go whenever you want. Whenever it fits your schedule the best."

I grin. "You are so getting lucky later."

"Why can't I get lucky now?"

"Because you have to open your present."

His gaze rakes over my body. "I'm staring at the present I want to open."

I shiver. "Hold that thought." I crawl over him to nab the present I picked out for him.

"What is it?"

"You have to open it to find out."

He slowly and ever so meticulously removes the wrapping paper without tearing it.

"What are you doing? We're not re-using the wrapping paper."

"Nope but watching you try to be patient is fun."

I growl at him. "You're mean."

"We're in the bed. I'm allowed to tease you in the bed."

Stupid sirens. He's right. We made the agreement after I nearly cracked my head open on the kitchen counter when I had enough of his teasing. No more teasing me anywhere I might get injured or end up kicking Jeremy in the balls.

He opens the box and frowns. "What is this?" He removes the old-fashioned nightcap and nightshirt. "You got me Scrooge pajamas?"

"You missed one thing."

He digs out the t-shirt and reads the front. "What part of bah-humbug don't you understand?"

I clap. "Isn't it perfect?"

He smiles as he places the item back in the box. "Thank you for the gift."

I burst into laughter. "It's a gag gift." I reach under the bed and bring out another package. "Here's a real gift, ya big whiner."

"I wasn't whining."

"No, but you were terrified I was going to make you wear the pajamas."

"More worried you had a fetish about old men."

I shiver. "Nope. The only fetish I have is for a billionaire with dirty blond hair and light brown eyes."

His eyes warm. "Good, since I have a fetish for a baker with bright blue eyes and a perky nose."

I tap his gift. "Open it."

This time, he doesn't torture me and tears into the package. This is the way Christmas presents should be opened. With abandon and glee.

"What?" His brow wrinkles as he stares at the plaque. It says *Jeremy's place.*

I remove the plaque from the tissue paper. "It'll be affixed to your table in the bakery so everyone knows it's your place."

"Princess," he mutters.

"What?" I bite my lip. "You don't like it?" I blow out a breath. "It was a silly idea."

I start to stand but he tackles me. "It's not a stupid idea. It's perfect. You're perfect. Thank you."

"You're serious? You like it?"

"I don't like it." My stomach falls. "I fucking love it. I love you."

I smile up at him. "And I love you. Happy first Christmas together."

"I can't wait to spend every Christmas with you."

"In your Scrooge pajamas."

"I don't give a fuck. I'd wear a tutu and reindeer antlers if it makes you smile. As long as I'm with you, I'm in."

I wrap my arms around him. "Thank you."

"Why are you thanking me?"

"I love Christmas but my Christmases haven't been very happy since I returned to Smuggler's Hideaway after culinary school. I was lonely, and my parents were dismissive of me."

And now here I am laying in bed with the man who loves me who I love. I've come a long way.

He places a finger over my lips. "Nope. We're not discussing unhappy thoughts while we're in this bed together."

I don't fight him. He's right. We should have a space where my parents can't invade. And the bed is as good a space as any.

I bat my eyelashes at him. "Whatever will we do instead?"

He nips my bottom lip. "I vote for unwrapping my favorite present."

"Another present? Someone's greedy."

"When it comes to you, I'm always greedy. I can't get enough of you."

"Good. Since I will never get enough of you."

He melds his lips to mine and I sigh. His taste of chocolate, espresso and sin hits me and I moan. I love how he tastes. It reminds me of baking, which is my favorite thing in the world. This man was made for me.

"I love you," he murmurs.

I used to think I had to earn love. Prove I was worthy of it with perfect grades, perfect cookies, perfect smiles. But Jeremy loves me messy and loud and ambitious. He's the first person who's ever made me feel I was *enough*.

"I'm thankful you couldn't work in the sauna at Eli's house. Maybe I should send him a gift basket as a thank you."

He grunts. "Gift baskets later. Remove clothes now."

"Bossy. Bossy."

"And you love it."

"I love you," I whisper.

He smiles, brushing my hair off my face like it's the most precious thing in the world. Like I'm the most precious thing in the world. "Then I'm the luckiest man alive."

I melt into him. The tree lights cast soft shadows across the room. Our first Christmas together. The first of forever.

About D.E. Haggerty

This page is for authors to share their bio with their readers. How it is written will depend on the genre you write as well as your desired relationship with your audience.

The Author bio page is usually written in third person and shares information about the author such as where they are from, what their hobbies and sources of inspiration are, how and why they became an author, or why they write the type of content they write.

Printed in Dunstable, United Kingdom